"You Never Got Any ~~~~~ Letters, Did You?"

Tony asked.

Susan's laugh was a half sob. "Does it somehow absolve you of your guilt feelings to pretend?"

He placed his hands on her shoulders and gently rocked her until she was forced to rest her hands on his chest for balance. She dropped her head wearily against his shoulder.

"Oh, Susan, what have we done to each other?" he asked softly.

She tried to push him away, but he held on, steadily tightening the pressure of his arms until she was standing close against him.

"It doesn't matter anymore," Susan said sadly. "It was all so long ago. It could have happened to two other people.

"But it didn't," Tony said fiercely. "It happened to us!"

Dear Reader:

SILHOUETTE DESIRE is an exciting new line of contemporary romances from Silhouette Books. During the past year, many Silhouette readers have written in telling us what other types of stories they'd like to read from Silhouette, and we've kept these comments and suggestions in mind in developing SILHOUETTE DESIRE.

DESIREs feature all of the elements you like to see in a romance, plus a more sensual, provocative story. So if you want to experience all the excitement, passion and joy of falling in love, then SILHOUETTE DESIRE is for you.

For more details write to:

Jane Nicholls
Silhouette Books
PO Box 236
Thornton Road
Croydon
Surrey CR9 3RU

ANNETTE BROADRICK
Bachelor Father

Silhouette Desire

Originally Published by Silhouette Books
division of
Harlequin Enterprises Ltd.

First published in Great Britain 1985
by Silhouette Books, 15–16 Brook's Mews, London W1A 1DR

© Annette Broadrick 1985

Silhouette, Silhouette Desire and Colophon are Trade Marks of Harlequin Enterprises B.V.

ISBN 0 373 05219 7

225–1185

Printed and bound in Great Britain by
Cox & Wyman Ltd, Reading

ANNETTE BROADRICK

a native Texan, lives in Missouri with her husband, Gaylen, his poodle and her Siamese cat. Now that her four sons are grown, she has decided to combine a lifelong addiction to reading romance fiction with her equally compulsive need to write.

Other Silhouette Books by Annette Broadrick

Silhouette Desire
Hunter's Prey

For further information about
Silhouette Books please write to:

Jane Nicholls
Silhouette Books
PO Box 236
Thornton Road
Croydon
Surrey CR9 3RU

To Dave, Rick, Randy and Kevin,
who taught me all I know about ten-year-old boys. . . .

1

The phone rang for a second time before Susan paused from reviewing the contract in front of her and absently reached for the jangling instrument.

"Susan McCormick." Her voice was carefully modulated to sound confident and professional, as befitted a competent corporate attorney.

"Mom! You'll never guess who was at school today!"

A warm smile appeared on her face and she glanced at the walnut-framed photograph on her desk. The smiling face of her exuberant ten-year-old son stared back at her, his black eyes filled with mischief, his curly dark brown hair falling over his forehead.

"Probably not, Steve," she responded with a chuckle. "So why don't you tell me?"

"Tony Antonelli! Can you believe it? The star left

fielder for the Atlanta Aces came to our school and spoke to us!"

For a moment Susan thought she was going to faint. Blood rushed from her head and dizziness overcame her. Tony was back in Santa Barbara. Her thoughts flew back to her childhood and she remembered black eyes sparkling in a tanned, laughing face, a white, dimpled smile flashing, unruly black curls tumbling over a forehead. Her thoughts flitted to her teen years and the bronzed male that could have been the inspiration of the Renaissance artists, his muscled arms and shoulders developed from years of playing sports of all kinds—especially baseball.

Tony—who had taught the young Susan to enjoy being young and alive, who'd given her her first taste of freedom and companionship and friendship, and later was responsible for her first lesson in how to survive the loss of a love.

"I bet that was really exciting, Steve," she heard herself saying faintly, her voice betraying her with a slight quiver.

"Yeah," her son responded with enthusiasm. "I had PE right after he spoke and we were playing baseball and I saw him talking to the coach and— Mom?"

"Yes, Steve?"

"How come you never told me you knew Tony Antonelli?" His tone bordered on accusation.

"How did you find out I did?"

"He told me."

Susan leaned back in her chair, helpless to combat

the whirling sensation she was feeling. "You talked to him," she stated in a calm voice while she watched her hand tremble against the arm of her chair.

She wasn't ready for this. She should have been given some warning. Some small voice should have told her when she got up that morning that this was not going to be a good day.

"How did you happen to be talking to him, Steve?" She didn't have to fake her interest. His answer was of vital importance to her.

"The coach called me over." His voice suddenly went up several notes. "I hit a triple and I guess Tony was watching or something. So when I crossed home plate he called me over."

"Sounds like you've licked your batting slump, doesn't it?"

"Yeah." He tried for nonchalance but couldn't quite carry it off. "The coach introduced me to Tony and when he heard my name was McCormick he told me he'd grown up with a Michael McCormick. I told him that was my dad's name and he said he grew up with you, too." His tone hardened. "Is that true, Mom?"

"Yes."

"Then why didn't you ever tell me? I didn't even know Tony was from Santa Barbara. You've never once mentioned his name!"

What could she say? She could hardly lie to him and say she hadn't thought he'd be interested. She knew him too well for that. Sports seemed to be his whole life. It had been hard for her to accept, but she'd slowly forced herself to face the fact that Steve didn't take after her as far as his interests were concerned. She didn't care for sports and Tony Antonelli had a great deal to do with her feelings on the subject.

Steve said something, but she didn't catch it—something about dinner. "What did you say?"

He groaned, impatient with her lack of attention. "I said that I invited him to have dinner with us tonight, since you guys are old friends and everything."

"Stephen Spencer McCormick! You did no such thing!" Never had Steve taken it upon himself to invite anyone to their home without checking with her first. And Tony, of all people!

Steve knew he was in trouble. His mother never used his full name. Never. He wasn't sure what its use portended, but he had a bad feeling about it.

"What's wrong, Mom?"

Susan no longer had to worry about dizziness. All of her blood had rushed back to her head, where it pounded in heavy waves of anger and fear. She did not ever want to see Tony Antonelli. He was part of her past and she wanted him to stay there.

She had to say something to Steve. She knew her reaction had alarmed him—it was so much out of character for her. Normally Susan remained calm and rational, her emotions carefully controlled.

"You don't invite someone to dinner without checking with me first, Steve, and you know it. How could you?"

Puzzled, Steve wasn't sure what to say. "But, Mom, he's a friend of yours."

"Hardly a friend. We just happened to live next door to each other while we were growing up." *Why was she denying their shared past? As some sort of protection?* She attempted to salvage the truth. "We haven't seen each other in years."

"I know. That's why I thought you'd want to see him now." Thinking to appease her, he added, "I've already told Hannah there'd be company for dinner. She didn't seem to mind."

"That's hardly the point." She paused, trying to calm down and to get a grip on her emotions. "I take it he accepted?" *What was she going to do?*

"Oh, yeah, he said he'd be here at seven."

Susan glanced at the large calendar hanging on the wall by her desk. "Steve, you *are* aware that today is the first Wednesday of the month, aren't you?"

Silence. Then a groan. "Oh, Mom, I forgot."

"Yes."

More silence. "Couldn't we call Grandmother and explain that something came up? I mean, we go over there all the time," he muttered with some exaggeration. "Would it really matter if we missed just this once?"

"What do you think?"

"Aw, Mom. I didn't do it on purpose. Honest. But Tony Antonelli, Mom! Maybe Grandmother would understand if we just explained—"

"No, your grandmother would not understand, believe me."

What were her choices, after all? Did she want Tony aware of how little desire she had to see him?

11

Did she want him to feel he had that much importance in her life? Of course not. On the other hand, was she ready to face her mother with yet another example of her shortcomings as a loving, dutiful daughter?

Her silence was more than a ten-year-old could handle. "What can we do?"

She could hear the hurt and dejection in his voice. Why should he be faced with a dilemma he couldn't understand?

"I'll call your grandmother and ask if we can visit her tomorrow night instead." Approaching the guillotine appealed to her more.

"Would you, Mom, would you really? Oh, that would be super. So you'll be home at the usual time, then?"

Wondering if she'd get any more work done during the rest of the afternoon, she nodded absently. "Yes, I'll be home by six."

Susan stared at the phone in its cradle long after she'd hung up. The most important thing for her to remember was not to let Steve know how upset she was. Somehow she would get through the evening. She would just have to concentrate on keeping her composure.

She pictured Tony the way he'd looked the last time she'd seen him. At twenty-one he'd been breathtaking, and the seventeen-year-old she'd been had been mesmerized by him. Unfortunately.

Susan shook her head in an effort to dispel the memories that had arrived with Steve's call. Deter-

mined to face her next unpleasant task with composure, she picked up the phone once again. She
dialed briskly and listened to the ring. Then a voice
answered.

"Hello, Claudine, is Mother around?"

"Just a moment, Susan."

Susan stared at Steve's picture, at the compelling
grin that caused everyone he met to smile back.
Meeting Tony was probably the most exciting thing
he could imagine happening to him. She refused to
allow her feelings to interfere with his enjoyment of
the evening.

"Susan?"

"Hello, Mother."

"Why are you calling?"

*Why don't you give me a chance to tell you,
Mother?* Pushing her resentment of her mother's
attitude to the back of her mind, Susan answered.
"I'm calling to let you know that Steve and I won't be
over for dinner this evening."

"Why must you shorten Stephen's distinguished
name with that slangy expression, Susan? If the
name is good enough for your father, it is certainly
good enough for your son."

"Yes, Mother."

"What do you mean, you aren't coming over
tonight? You know we expect you on the first
Wednesday of each month."

"I know, Mother. That's why I called. Could we
make it tomorrow night instead?"

"You know very well my bridge club meets on

13

Thursday afternoons, Susan. I am absolutely exhausted by evening."

"Of course, Mother. It just slipped my mind."

"Why can't you come tonight?"

"Stephen"—Susan emphasized the name slightly, the only sign she gave that she'd been holding on to her temper with a firm grip—"invited a friend over for dinner tonight. He'd forgotten what day it is."

"Which friend is that?"

"Why do you ask?"

"Well, I certainly hope you've met all of Stephen's friends, Susan. When you refused to allow him to go to private school, I warned you how little control you'd have over the type of person he meets."

Please, dear Lord, give me strength. "I'll be sure to have his friend bring his pedigree, Mother, which I will check over very carefully before allowing him to enter our home."

"Is that supposed to be funny?"

"Not really, Mother."

"Good, because I do not find it amusing. And I think you are being most inconsiderate to cancel this late in the day. Claudine will undoubtedly be most upset."

I doubt that very much, Mother. "Please give her our apologies." Noting the time, she asked, "Then we'll see you next month?" Her tone betrayed her impatience.

"No, wait a moment, Susan. I'll make a trade with you. I'll forgive you for not showing up tonight if you'll come for dinner on Friday instead."

Suspicious as to why her mother was so willing to

14

concede the issue, she asked, "What's happening this Friday night?"

"Oh, Edwin and Lorraine are back from Europe and we're having them over for dinner."

Edwin and Lorraine were the biggest bores Susan had ever had the misfortune of meeting. Her mother found them fascinating and, as usual, no one seemed to know how her father felt about them. Stephen Spencer was always unfailingly polite, but gave nothing of his thoughts away. She wished she knew how he did it. One of these days, if she were ever able to get him alone, Susan was determined to ask him how he put up with her mother and her mother's friends.

"Mother, I'd rather not, if you don't mind. I have a heavy schedule in the office that day and—"

"It is rare that I ask anything of you, Susan, and you know it. I wouldn't ask now if Lorraine's nephew weren't coming with them. I really do need the extra person at the table to even out the numbers."

"You could always have Claudine eat with you, when she wasn't serving, of course." Silence. *Oh, dear. I've gone too far.* With a sigh of unwilling acceptance, Susan asked, "What time should I be there on Friday, Mother?"

More silence. *Ah, yes, I remember this treatment well. For years you managed to intimidate me, Mother, but now I've discovered that silence works just as well for me.*

The wire hummed in the background as the two strong-willed women waited each other out. Susan began to read the contract before her. She was

15

tempted to put the call on the speaker phone while she waited but decided she'd done enough for one day.

A long-suffering sigh eventually drifted along the wire. "Dinner will be at eight o'clock, Susan. If you think you can be polite and not insult anyone, you might wish to come at seven-thirty, to meet Harry."

"To meet who?"

"Harry Brulanger, Lorraine's nephew."

"Oh. Fine, then. I'll see you on Friday."

Replacing the phone, Susan picked up the contract once more, eager to bury her thoughts in the familiar legal terms, hoping to blot out the recent conversation from her mind.

Tony Antonelli looked around the hotel suite with disgust. He was sick of staying in hotels. After his mother's death five years before, he'd sold the home he'd bought for her. He'd moved around so much, he hadn't known where he wanted to settle, so he'd rented apartments for years.

No more. He was back home now. The season was over and he was tired. He'd come back to Santa Barbara to look around for property. He might buy a condo on the beach. He didn't know what he wanted anymore.

He stood before the bathroom mirror knotting his tie. He hated the damn things. However, he was determined to show Susan and her son that he, too, could look and act like a gentleman. He gave an unamused laugh. Not that it would matter. Susan had long ago made it clear how she felt about him.

He wondered how she'd react to the discovery that her son looked at him as though he expected him to take off in the air any moment to fight crime and preserve truth, justice and the American way.

Tony grabbed his hairbrush and once again tried to force his black curls into some semblance of order. As soon as he brushed them back they immediately fell forward across his forehead. *What the hell.* He threw the brush down. He caught the glitter in his eyes and looked away with disgust. *You're excited about seeing her again, you stupid fool. You'll never learn.*

Susan Spencer was the only woman he'd ever wanted to marry. He couldn't remember when he first fell in love with her. It seemed as though he'd always loved her, and like a fool he'd believed she felt the same way. He could still feel the terrible pain of discovering that even at seventeen she had known what she wanted, and it hadn't been he.

She'd taught him a valuable lesson. In the eleven years since he'd faced the fact that all of her protestations of love had been lies, he'd never been tempted to risk being played for a fool again. He'd never lacked for female companions, but he never intended to marry any of them.

He was glad his mother never discovered his feelings. She had often talked of the day when he would settle down, marry and have a family. He felt another twinge of pain. Yes, he'd wanted children. He and Susan had talked about what kind of family they would have. They had decided to have four children, he remembered with a slight smile, as though they could make plans and they would all materialize just as they wished. Only it hadn't worked out that way. He'd been someone for her to tease and torment until Michael decided to marry her. He just wished he'd understood before he'd gotten so involved with her.

He wondered what she looked like now. Her son said she was an attorney. He had trouble picturing her in a law office counseling clients. How did she wear her hair these days? He could remember the fine blond hair, bleached by the hot southern California sun, hanging in rippling waves down the straight column of her spine. Of course that was only when she managed to escape from her dragon of a mother. Otherwise she had worn it in prim braids wrapped around her head.

He wondered if her eyes were still the color of turquoise, so clear he had always felt he was looking into the depths of her soul when he looked into them. Her skin had always glowed, golden with the perpetual touch of the sun. She'd been beautiful, even as a child. By sixteen she'd taken his breath away. Fat lot of good that had done him. He'd been the son of the next door neighbor's housekeeper.

He admitted to himself that she and Michael had never seemed to care about his background when they were growing up together. Because he'd been three years older than Michael and four years older than Susan, they had looked up to him and followed his lead. He grinned at some of his memories. He'd thought up some great adventures over the years and they'd gamely followed him, taking their scoldings from their respective parents courageously, but always willing to follow him again.

He'd been sorry to hear about Michael's death four years ago. What a waste. Michael had been a musical genius, a child prodigy. Perhaps that was one of the reasons the two of them had been so close. Everybody else had treated Michael like a freak. He'd loved Michael like a brother and had been ripped apart by the news of his sudden death. Leukemia had taken him at twenty-four. Tony glared into the mirror. How ironic that Michael should be the one to go, with all of his musical talent, while a jock like himself was as healthy as a horse.

He picked up his suit coat from the bed and shrugged into it, trying to halt his unchecked memories. Even now, he still had feelings of inadequacy that assailed him whenever he recalled his past. Because of his careful investments over the years, he was confident he was the financial equal of the McCormicks and the Spencers, but whenever he returned to Santa Barbara he once again became the son of the McCormicks' housekeeper.

He tugged the hotel room door closed behind him and strode toward the elevators. He didn't know why he'd agreed to this dinner anyway. There was something in the boy's eyes that had pleaded with him and he couldn't say no. Tonight would be his final visit to the past. He wanted no reminders.

Susan McCormick never dithered. She was a calm, resolute woman who made a decision after carefully considering all known factors, then refused to waste a moment worrying over the correctness of her decision—which was why she was unnerved to discover she couldn't decide what to wear for dinner.

She first thought she should appear tailored and businesslike. After all, this dinner was for Steve's sake anyway. She had put on her gray suit and was coiling her hair on the nape of her neck when Steve paused by her door.

"Mom! You aren't going to dress like a lawyer for dinner, are you?" He stood in the doorway of her room, his hands on his hips, his face wearing an expression of disgust. "Why can't you put on something pretty for a change?"

The disappointment in his eyes convicted her.

However, when she put on her sheer pink dress with the swirling skirt and full sleeves, she wasn't at all certain her choice had been the right one. Would he think she was dressing up to impress him? Then again, what was wrong with looking feminine and desirable? She glanced into the mirror, undecided. Perhaps it would be better to put her hair in a coil, as she had earlier planned, rather than having it fall to her shoulders.

Susan heard the doorbell and knew she didn't have time to redo her hair. He had arrived. She stepped into her matching pink sandals with the three-inch heels. At five feet four inches, Susan wanted desperately to look tall and slender tonight. She would have to settle for slender, she supposed with a sigh. After one last glance in the mirror, she walked down the hall.

Tony almost didn't recognize her. Where was the sparkling young girl with the flashing eyes and golden skin? This woman was too thin and pale. Was she ill? The thought caused a shock of pain to shoot through him, making a mockery of his earlier thoughts about her. His feelings for Susan had always been too intense for either of them to handle. Nothing seemed to have changed for him in that respect.

He held out his hand. "Good to see you again, Susan."

She stared at him in confusion. This wasn't the Tony Antonelli Susan remembered—in jeans, sneakers and a sweatshirt. He bore no resemblance to the ballplayer she'd seen pictures of, either. Instead, he looked like one of the many businessmen she dealt with daily. He also loomed broader, larger than she remembered him. There was no trace of the boy of her memories. Susan wasn't at all certain she could treat the man with the necessary aloof politeness she'd planned. She could feel her heart beating erratically as she tried to adjust her mental picture to the reality.

She placed her hand in his, and immediately recognized her mistake. The warm, callused hand sent a tingling through her and she resigned herself to the knowledge that Tony would always have an effect on her that she wouldn't be able to control.

"It's good to see you, too, Tony," she responded. "May I get you something to drink?"

"Yes, please. Bourbon and water would be fine."

She moved away from him gratefully and walked over to the bar, keeping her back to him as she tried to steady the trembling in her hands. He mustn't see how he affected her.

Steve, unaware of the undercurrents, took over. "I saw you in the World Series, Tony. You were really great."

Tony turned to look at the boy and smiled. "Thank you, Steve."

Steve dropped his head for a moment, then looked up at the man with a shy smile. "I guess you hear that a lot, huh?"

Tony grinned. "Some. But that's okay. It's always nice to hear."

Susan handed Tony his drink and motioned to one of the sofas arranged before the large fireplace. Tony sat down and Susan sat across from him, while Steve, too excited to sit, paced around the room.

Tony gestured toward the large picture sitting on the mantel. "When was that taken?"

Susan glanced at the portrait of her, Michael, and Steve. In a low tone she answered, "Five years ago." She knew without looking what Tony saw—Michael smiling serenely into the camera, his light brown hair combed to the side, his gray eyes filled with good humor, while Susan sat in the curve of his arm, her smile radiant, as though she were amused by something the photographer said. Steve, at five, stared into the camera with a mischievous grin, his curly hair tumbling over his forehead. Susan had chosen that particular proof because of the expression on

Steve's face. His eyes had sparkled, as though he knew something the rest of them didn't. As it turned out, that was correct. Just as the picture was snapped the photographer stepped back solidly on a cat's tail, creating quite a commotion. Only Steve had noticed the cat wake up earlier and descend from its perch on a chair to begin licking its paws, directly behind the photographer.

She loved that particular expression of his; it epitomized how much he enjoyed life and everything around him.

"I was sorry to hear about Michael, Susan. By the time I got the news it was too late to get back for the funeral."

Susan stared into his glittering black eyes and wondered if that were true. Would he have come? It was no longer important.

"It was a shock to all of us. We had no warning he was that ill." She took a sip of her drink. "He'd been playing with the Los Angeles Symphony for two years and was doing very well. He'd also been working on some compositions of his own."

Hannah, a solidly built woman of indeterminate age, appeared at the arched entryway between the living room and dining area. "Dinner is ready whenever you are, Susan," she announced.

Susan glanced up. "Thanks, Hannah. I want you to meet Tony." Starting toward the dining area, Susan paused at her housekeeper's side. Glancing over at Tony, she said, "Hannah Stilling, Tony Antonelli."

Hannah smiled. "I knew who you were, of course. Your coming to dinner has been all Steve could talk about since he got home from school."

She radiated good humor. Tony was amused at Susan's attitude. She treated Hannah more as family than as hired help. He wondered what her mother thought of that. "I'm very glad to meet you, Hannah. Have you been with Susan long?"

She nodded. "Ever since Steve was born. I was hired to keep him while Susan went to school."

Tony glanced at Susan. Why was she looking at him with such apprehension? Did she think he might snub the woman? That was a laugh, considering his background.

"You've set only three places, Hannah. Which one of us isn't supposed to eat tonight?" Susan asked with a grin.

"Me," Hannah responded. "I ate earlier because I wanted to watch a program on PBS that starts in a few minutes. I thought you might be able to look after yourselves just this once."

Susan laughed. "We'll try to manage without you, but it won't be easy."

Tony could never remember later what they'd eaten that evening. He found himself joining into the conversation, telling stories to Steve about some of the antics he and his mother and father used to pull, while Susan laughingly protested that he didn't need any more ideas—Steve came up with plenty on his own.

Steve began to lose his awe of Tony and started

asking him pertinent questions about baseball, some of the players and batting techniques. Tony soon realized the boy was highly intelligent and well-versed in the sport. The intelligence didn't surprise him, but the love of baseball did. Although Michael and Susan had willingly tagged along after him, neither one of them had shown much interest or aptitude in sports.

Tony watched as Steve explained something to his mother he'd recently seen on television. It was obvious to the most casual observer that Susan and her son were very close. He wondered if Steve had spent much time with his father.

"Were you ever in Boy Scouts, Tony?" Steve asked.

"As a matter of fact, I was. Why?"

In a careful, offhand manner, Steve answered, "Because I'm a Boy Scout and we have an all-day hiking trip planned in a couple of weeks." Steve darted a glance at his mother, then quickly looked back at Tony. "You could come along as my guest, if you want. All the other guys are bringing their dads."

"Stephen!" Susan's shocked tone echoed around the room. He looked at her with a mixture of apology and defiance.

"He can always say no, Mom. It's no big deal."

Here was one young man who wasn't being brow-beaten by a possibly overprotective mother, Tony decided. "Exactly when is this all-day hiking trip planned, Steve?"

"Saturday, the eighteenth. We're going to meet at

Mr. Spangler's house at seven in the morning." He was unable to meet Tony's gaze.

"I'm sure Tony has better things to do than go hiking, Steve," Susan managed to interject.

"On the contrary," Tony drawled. "I think it sounds like fun. You've got yourself a date."

Steve sat there for a moment, stunned. Never in his wildest dreams had he considered that Tony would actually go with him. He wasn't even sure why he'd asked him. Now that he had an acceptance, he didn't know what to say. He managed to choke out, "That's swell," and then took a large drink of milk.

"I thought you had to be ten to be in Scouts. Or are you a Cub Scout?" Tony asked.

Steve looked up in surprise. "No, I'm a Boy Scout, and I'm ten."

Tony sat staring at Steve. "You're ten?" he asked, his muscles tensing as a suspicion suddenly gripped him.

"Yes, sir. I was ten on February seventh."

Tony sat there as though a bomb had exploded on the table before him. *February? Exactly nine months after he left Santa Barbara?*

Steve couldn't understand it. Why did Tony look so upset? His face had darkened and his eyes seemed to be shooting sparks.

Tony's gaze clashed with Susan's. "How very interesting. Imagine my not knowing that."

Susan refused to look away. "It never occurred to us you'd be interested, Tony."

He sat there, stunned by the information he'd just received, stunned by the implications, then caught the bewildered expression on Steve's face. Forcing himself to relax, he attempted a smile at the puzzled boy. "I didn't even know you existed, Steve, until I read about your father's death."

It was Susan's turn to look bewildered. "You mean Mama Angelina never told you about Steve?"

His look barely concealed the contempt he felt. "I doubt very much Mama ever knew about his existence."

"That's not true! Steve and I used to visit your mother often when he was little. She was lonesome in that big house you bought her—never felt very comfortable with the neighbors. Steve loved to go visit her."

Steve blurted out, "You mean Mama Angelina was your mother, Tony?" Never had he found an adult conversation more confusing.

Tony's head was whirling, his thoughts zooming around his head in a kaleidoscopic display of confused images. His mother had known about Steve and had never told him? He stared at the boy before him, taking in the darkness of his eyes and hair, the same unruly mop of curls that caused him so much trouble. How could he have missed it? How could anyone who knew him? Was that why his mother had never told him?

When Tony didn't answer Steve's question, Susan responded. "That's right, Steve. I guess I never mentioned that to you."

Steve looked at the two adults with dismay. "It seems to me there's a lot you haven't told me."

Tony looked at her with an identical expression. "So it would seem." Two pairs of black eyes filled with accusation stared at her. She was definitely not ready for this.

Susan hastily shoved her chair back and stood. "If everyone is finished, how does ice cream sound for dessert?" She gave Tony a look that pleaded for understanding. Couldn't he see they couldn't discuss it now?

Apparently he recognized her concern and agreed. She watched as he unclenched his fists and visibly relaxed his shoulders. "That sounds fine. How about you?" he asked Steve.

The adults seemed to be changing the subject, which was all right with him. He shrugged. "Sure, sounds great."

When she returned with the ice cream Susan was forced to keep the conversation going. Tony had withdrawn and made no effort to contribute more than an occasional answer to her questions. Only with Steve did he come out of his self-imposed silence. She was relieved when dinner was over and she excused herself to clear the table.

When she returned to the living room, Tony immediately stood. "I'm going to have to be going." He saw Steve's expression fall and frowned. "I'm sorry, Steve, but I promised to meet a friend later."

Steve tried for nonchalance. "Sure, I understand. I know you're busy."

"Not too busy to forget that hike, though."

Steve's expression wavered. "You mean you'll still go with me?"

Tony rested his hand on the boy's shoulder. "I wouldn't miss it, champ. I'm hoping you and I can get much better acquainted." He caught Susan's gaze with a level one of his own. "I intend to settle in Santa Barbara. There's no reason why I can't spend time with you and Steve, is there?"

A sharp pain caught Susan in the chest, as though his words were stilettos piercing her skin. The look he gave her challenged her and she wasn't ready to face that challenge at the moment. "We'll see," she murmured in as noncommittal a fashion as possible.

"That we will, old friend." He turned and grinned down at Steve. "You were right. Hannah's a great cook. You're very lucky."

That was all the encouragement Steve needed. "You'll have to come over again some time," he offered with the expansive graciousness of a good host.

Susan fought to hide her negative reaction to Steve's suggestion. She didn't want to discourage the hospitable part of his nature, but found herself wishing he'd practice on someone else.

"I'd like to see you tomorrow, Susan. How about lunch?"

His request caught her off guard. "Uh, I don't think so, Tony. I have a rather full day scheduled."

He smiled, but the smile never reached his eyes. "We really need to get together and catch up on old times, you know."

Had there been an implied threat in his remark?

There was nothing he could do to her, absolutely nothing, *except hurt Steve. He's already aware of my vulnerability where my son is concerned.*

She raised her chin slightly. "We don't have anything to discuss. Eleven years is a long time."

He stared at her, incredulous. "On the contrary. I believe we have a great deal to catch up on." He stopped, noting the bewilderment on Steve's face at his harsh tone. He reached over and ruffled the dark, unruly curls on Steve's head, a sudden sharp pain constricting his chest. *Susan has a great deal to answer for. One point I intend to find out—why I've had to wait all these years for some explanation.*

Tony opened the door, then paused, catching Susan's attention with a long, intent stare. "I'll call you."

Her small nod signaled Susan's reluctant acceptance of the inevitable.

She watched him walk down the long, curving walkway from her condominium to his low-slung sports car parked by the curb. She'd had a reprieve, but she knew she would have to be prepared to answer his questions. Why should she feel guilty? He was the one who'd left, not her. He was the one who'd never cared enough to find out if there had been any repercussions to their last evening together.

She closed the door and slowly walked down the hall to her bedroom. She owed him no explanation. She owed him nothing.

Then why had she felt like wrapping her arms around his lean waist and holding him close when she saw the first flash of pain on his face as the truth had hit him?

Susan's deeply buried feelings for Tony Antonelli had suddenly appeared from nowhere after all these years. She had honestly thought she was over him. It had taken only a few short hours in his presence to bring all of them tumbling back.

2

Susan lay in the darkness of her bedroom, staring at the shadows on the wall caused by the security lamp outside her condominium.

She reviewed the events of the evening and recognized a certain sense of inevitability about what had happened. Now that Tony was back, she realized it had been only a question of time anyway. The older Steve grew, the more he looked like Tony.

Tony had been Steve's age the first time she ever saw him.

She and Michael had been playing in the gazebo in the elaborate gardens Marsha Spencer took such pride in displaying. They'd both been told to go out and play but not to get dirty, an admonition that greatly limited their choice of entertainment. She would never forget the moment when she looked up from watching Michael building a skyscraper out of his construction set and saw Tony watching them, a slight frown on his face. At that moment Susan was convinced she'd never seen a more beautiful person. The smooth bronzed complexion caused a spurt of envy as she glanced down at her pale arms and legs. His black curls glistened with a vitality sadly lacking in her fine straight hair.

When Michael saw him, he stood up and walked over to him.

"Hi. I'm Michael. This is Susan. Do you want to help us build a city?"

Tony's startlingly black eyes looked first at Michael, then shifted to Susan. "Is that all there is to do around here?"

Michael shrugged. "I dunno. What do *you* want to do?"

Tony glanced around at the elaborate gardens. "Doesn't anyone play ball in this neighborhood?"

Susan remained silent as she waited for Michael to answer. "What kind of ball?"

"Any kind. Baseball, football, soccer."

"We don't have anything to play with."

Tony had slumped against the door frame, but straightened at Michael's remark. "I have a bat, ball, and a couple of gloves. How about some batting practice?"

Michael glanced over at Susan, hesitation plain on his face. Susan stood up, smoothing the wrinkles from her playsuit.

"That sounds like fun," she said. "Where can we play?"

Tony glanced over the hedge into the neatly clipped lawn next door. "How about over there?"

That had been the beginning of their friendship. Tony explained he was the son of Angelina Antonelli, who'd just been hired as housekeeper for the Mc-Cormicks. He and his mother had moved into the apartment located over the three-car garage.

He didn't seem to mind spending his time with the younger children, which endeared him to them. He found games to play that stretched and taxed them, but were never beyond their ability. Unfortunately, they quickly discovered it was impossible to spend time with Tony and stay clean.

Their first day together set the pattern of their relationship. Susan took her turn chasing batted balls and tried desperately to catch a ball coming toward her. Running backward and leaping high to catch it, she lost her balance and fell into the goldfish pond. The water wasn't deep, but it was brackish and she climbed out with slimy water and mud all over her. Her neat pigtails had degenerated into a wild tangle of dripping hair.

It was unfortunate that Susan attempted to sneak into the house just as Marsha Spencer was showing her garden club members the flower beds. Susan would never forget the look of horror on her mother's face, nor the amusement on the faces of her mother's guests. She'd been banished to her room without supper and without regard to the scraped knee that needed attention.

Susan couldn't remember the name of the house-keeper at the time, but she remembered her gentle scolding and compassion as she helped Susan to strip and get into the tub, and her gentle ministrations later. She'd even smuggled some dinner up to her that night in rebellion against Marsha's edict, which was probably why she hadn't lasted very long.

Even at six Susan knew better than to tell her mother about Tony. It was at that point in her life that she became quite protective of him where her mother was concerned. She never spoke his name, nor made any reference to him.

It wasn't long until Marsha discovered for herself who was luring the two quiet children into disobeying their parents, and she began to wage a battle to keep Susan away from Tony, even suggesting to the McCormicks that they dismiss Angelina. Susan was always grateful to the McCormicks for refusing to bow down to Marsha, which caused a distinct cooling of the friendship between the two families. The ensuing lack of communication further assisted the three children to spend time together without Marsha discovering what they were doing. As long as Susan would announce she was going to see Michael, she had her mother's full permission and approval. It didn't occur to Marsha that the two children were disregarding her rules by spending all their free time with Tony.

Whenever Susan read stories about the perfect male, she always pictured Tony. His body was a well-honed instrument trained to do what he wanted it to do. What he wanted it to do was to play baseball and he did that very well, indeed.

When he graduated from high school, Tony received a baseball scholarship to attend the University of California at Los Angeles. He seldom came home because he was also working part-time to help with the finances.

Mama Angelina was very proud of him.

She'd always been Mama Angelina to Michael and Susan—she was the mother Susan had secretly wished she'd had, though she refused to acknowledge the sacrilegious thought aloud. It was with Mama Angelina that Susan shared her small triumphs and tears, her first boyfriend, her first formal. It was Mama Angelina who could talk with her about Tony to Susan's heart's content.

Susan was fifteen when Tony first asked her for a date. It was the first time Susan couldn't ask Mama Angelina's advice. He'd invited her to a movie. It was summer and he was working full-time at a service station not far from their home. She'd missed him so much during the year and wanted to spend time with him, yet she knew her mother would never allow it.

It was then Susan began the deception that was to trap her later. She told her mother she had a date with Michael. Her mother lectured her on how young both of them were, but in the end didn't refuse to let her go. Susan, being her usual direct self, immediately found Michael and told him what she had done. He thought it was funny. He also agreed not to give her away.

Susan spent as much time with Tony as he chose to give her that summer. He was casual, but seemed to like being with her. While Michael was involved with special lessons at the conservatory, Susan went with Tony to local ballgames, watching as he played on the city league. It was a very beautiful, very innocent summer for them.

By the time another year rolled around, there had been several changes for both of them. Susan had been slow in developing, but that year her slender body began to show the soft curves of ripening womanhood. Her face had lost the roundness of childhood and her eyes, with their slight slant at the corners, had become mysterious pools of blue staring out at the world.

Susan would never forget the morning she discovered Tony was back home for the summer. She'd burst into the garage apartment to show Mama Angelina something now long since forgotten. Tony was in the kitchen with nothing on but a skin-tight pair of cutoff jeans, his hair rumpled from sleep.

"Tony!"

He glanced around from pouring a cup of coffee, then stared in surprise, absently setting the pot down. "Susan?"

She laughed, delighted to see him. "I didn't know you were home. When did you get here?"

He continued to stare at her in the shorts and halter she used as a summer uniform. "Late last night."

"It must have been. I didn't think I could sleep through the sound of your car. You must have gotten a new muffler on it."

He grinned. "As a matter of fact, I did, brat. You should show that car a little more respect, you know. It's older than you are." He turned back to the counter and without looking at her asked, "Do you want a cup of coffee?"

"Sure, but I came over to see if Mama Angelina was here."

Still with his back to her, Tony replied, "No, she took the car and went shopping. I don't know when she'll be back."

Susan had known Tony for ten years by that time and during those years had seen him in various states of undress. She couldn't understand why the sight of his bare back should affect her so. She only knew it did. His shoulders were broad and heavily muscled, and his spine was indented, forming a slender valley down his back to disappear into the low-hanging cutoffs. She had a strong urge to run her hand down that slight indentation, to feel the muscles that seemed to ripple just below the skin.

She was still staring when he turned around with her cup of coffee. They were a few feet apart and she looked at him as though mesmerized. She saw a flame suddenly spark in his dark eyes and he closed the distance between them. His gaze fell on her soft lips, and she self-consciously licked them, remembering she had dashed over before bothering with any makeup. Suddenly shy, she dropped her gaze and took the offered cup.

"So how did you do in school this year? Are you going to be a senior in the fall?" Tony's voice sounded relaxed, although she wondered at the slight drawl, as though he were teasing her. She nodded, still watching her coffee.

"Me, too, although I'm not sure I'm going back."

She glanced up, startled. "What do you mean?"

He grinned. "I think I may get an offer to play professionally. If I do, I'm not going to wait to graduate. I'm going for it now."

"But, Tony, you'll need your degree to get a job."

"If I become a pro, Susan my sweet, I'll have the job I want for several years to come."

"That isn't a career, Tony. That's just a hobby."

"Maybe so, but it's helped to pay for my college education, and if I'm good enough, it may pay my way for several years."

She stared at him, amazed. She'd never thought about being able to make money by playing ball. Every man she knew worked in some type of business. Her father ran the family firm and, being an only child, Susan had begun to think about learning how to take over when he retired. She'd already begun to map out her college curriculum, and was interested in the possibility of a pre-law course. A good businessman needed to know the ins and outs of the law, or so she decided.

"Don't you have any ambition to become successful?"

Tony stared at her for a moment, then raised his cup to his lips. After a moment he shrugged. "I suppose we need to define the word *success*. We probably have different ideas as to the meaning." He glanced out the window. "But it's too nice a morning to waste on a philosophical discussion. Why don't we go play some tennis?"

Tony and Susan spent their free time together that summer, but there was a difference in the relationship she could never quite understand. Tony didn't seem as relaxed around her as before. It seemed to Susan he went out of his way not to touch her. Before he had always taken her hand to guide her, or draped an arm around her shoulder. Now he was very polite about opening doors, but he never came close to her. And she missed his touch. She found that many of her dreams were about him, and in all of them just as he would start to put his arms around her, she'd wake up.

What was wrong? She'd never had the nerve to ask him for fear she wouldn't like the answer. She would have been more upset if he'd been seeing someone else, but she knew he wasn't. He still seemed to want her around, but only at a slight distance.

They didn't see much of Michael that summer. A couple of times he joined them for a hamburger and once went to the movies with them. He seemed to be involved in his music and content to live in his own world. Susan hadn't realized how far they'd drifted apart, and she felt a sharp jab at the loss. She loved Michael, but she didn't miss him as she did Tony when he was at school. All of her dreams and desires seemed to revolve around Tony, but she knew Michael was there if she ever needed him.

Tony ended up returning to school his final year after all, and their last evening together that summer forever changed their relationship.

Susan stirred restlessly, her thoughts a torment. She had pushed them to a corner of her mind, where they had been content to stay until Tony stepped into her life once more. She didn't know how she was going to be able to cope with his presence now. She closed her eyes, willing herself to sleep. Instead, her thoughts drifted once again to the last summer she and Tony had spent together.

She remembered she'd gone to a ballgame in which he was playing, and several of his teammates and their girlfriends had decided to go to the beach afterward. They had all piled into various cars and driven to Piedmont Park. There was a full moon, which brightened the beach so that they needed no artificial light. The fire that was built gave off a cheery glow and they all enjoyed the quiet of the moonlight and the soft sighs of the waves.

They sat around the fire, laughing and talking, and Susan was surprised when Tony suddenly stood up and pulled her up with him. "Let's go for a walk."

She was pleased to have a few minutes alone with him. It had been hard for her to ignore the fact that he was leaving the next day. He seemed to think nothing of it. He'd left to return to school each fall and she'd never seemed to care before. Susan admitted to herself she didn't understand why she was upset now. However, she knew there would be an empty place in her life and she wasn't at all sure how to fill the void.

Tony surprised her once again by pulling her close to his side and leaning over to whisper into her ear. "I'm going to miss you, Susan my sweet. I've been thinking about bundling you in with my clothes and taking you with me."

His arm felt warm around her shoulders, so why

should his words cause a slight shiver to run down her spine? She looked up at him uncertainly. "I'm going to miss you, too."

He stopped and turned her to face him. "Is that why you've had such a long face tonight? I thought you must be bored with the game."

She grinned. "How could I be bored when you hit two home runs and a triple. Surely you heard me screaming."

"Oh, was that you? I thought it was a siren going off somewhere."

She doubled her fist and poked him in the ribs. "Very funny, Antonelli. You trying to make it as a comedian in case you don't get picked up as a ballplayer?"

He pulled her closer to him, looping his arms behind her. "Something like that," he murmured.

He stood with his back to the light, so that Susan couldn't make out the expression on his face, but his husky tone caused a tingling feeling inside her. She glanced up at him. He lowered his head until his mouth brushed hers, but stopped when she stiffened in his arms.

"Hey, what's the matter, haven't you ever been kissed before?"

She attempted a nonchalant shrug. "Sure," she lied. "Lots of times."

He brushed his lips across hers once again. "Do you have something against my kissing you?" he whispered.

She shook her head, her voice suddenly gone.

Even now, Susan recalled her initiation into the sensual world with quickened breathing. He'd been so gentle with her, coaxing her to respond to him. As she relaxed against him, he began to explore her mouth with tender persistence until her lips parted slightly in a soft sigh. He slipped his tongue between them, playfully pursuing her tongue until she pulled away from him, trying to get her breath.

"Are you certain you've been kissed before?" he asked in a teasing whisper.

"Not like that!" She felt as though she'd been running and couldn't catch her breath. All her fantasies about Tony seemed to be coming true, and she wasn't sure she was ready for the reality.

He caught her to him, softly stroking her back. "I'm sorry, honey. I didn't mean to frighten you."

Susan buried her head in his shoulder. "You didn't frighten me," she admitted.

He laughed. "Good. Then you won't mind repeating the lesson. We might as well practice until we get it right."

Eventually they returned to the fire, where no one seemed to have missed them. Susan knew that those few minutes on the beach had changed her, awakening her to her own body and its needs. Nothing would ever be the same.

Tony came home for Thanksgiving. Normally he stayed in Los Angeles and worked through the holidays. Their first evening together took up where their last evening left off—in each other's arms.

"I want you to marry me, Susan," Tony managed to say as he forced himself to put some distance between them.

Susan stared up at him with shining eyes. "Oh, Tony, I never dreamed you really wanted to marry me. I love you so much." She sighed. "But I have to finish school, and I still have college ahead of me."

"Marriage won't stop you from getting your education. I'll see to that. There's been enough interest shown in me that I know I'll be picked up next spring. We'll have enough money to do anything we want!"

They sat curled up together in the front seat of his car, the waves on the nearby beach playing a background symphony to their conversation.

"Mother will never agree to my getting married so young."

"That isn't it at all, and you know it. You'll never be old enough to marry me."

"Well, you have to admit it's going to be a shock to her. She doesn't even know we've been seeing each other."

"She can't be that much of an ostrich, Susan. Do you mean to tell me she still thinks you're seeing Michael?"

"Yes."

"When are you going to tell her the truth?"

"I'm not sure."

"Well, it might be a good idea to mention who the groom's going to be so she won't faint at the wedding, don't you think?"

"Do we have to think about it now, Tony?" she asked as she curled her arms tighter around his neck. His soft moan as he found her lips was a very satisfactory answer.

During Christmas break Tony insisted on giving her an engagement ring. She reluctantly took it, but explained she would wear it on her finger only when she was with him. The rest of the time she wore it on a chain around her neck.

Not that he blamed her. She was only seventeen, after all, still in high school, and had never shown the least amount of rebellion toward her mother's rules, except for seeing him. He knew she loved him, just as he loved her, but it was going to take her time to break the strings her mother had so carefully tied to her.

It took all of his willpower not to initiate her more deeply into the loving side of her nature. She was so spontaneous with him and so very trusting, but he refused to take advantage of her innocence.

An unusually warm May evening found Susan arriving home about eleven. She'd spent the day with a couple of girlfriends at the beach, working on her tan. The evening was spent sharing their plans for the summer.

Susan hadn't told anyone how serious she was about Tony. Perhaps it was because it didn't seem quite real to her. She knew she loved him, but she could never picture her mother giving in to her marrying before college. However, she knew that when Tony got home in a few weeks he would insist on their setting a wedding date.

The thought of being married to him, actually married, set off tiny explosions of feeling within her every time she thought about it. If she could just keep that thought in mind, she was sure she could face her mother with calm determination.

Her friends let her off at the end of her driveway, and she had almost reached the sidewalk when she heard a voice.

"Susan?" A low-voiced shadow moved toward her. She recognized Tony's broad shoulders and lithe stride.

"Tony! You're home!" She ran to him, throwing her arms around him. "When did you get here? What are you doing here so soon? I thought you had another two weeks!" Her words tumbled over themselves as she kissed him repeatedly on his chin and jaw line.

"Where have you been?" His voice sounded harsh. He took her hand in a firm grip.

A faint light from the streetlamp cast shadows across his face. She strained to see his eyes, but had no trouble recognizing the frown that furrowed his brow. "The beach, why?"

Tony took her past the flagstones that led to her front door. Instead, they continued down the driveway and toward the gazebo. "Who were you with?"

Susan's amazement became tinged with irritation. "What difference does it make? I already have a father, Tony." She planted her heels, refusing to enter the gazebo.

Tony faced her, moonlight etching his features. His wry smile echoed the sheepish tone as he responded. "You're right, honey. It's just that I've been waiting around to see you for hours."

Bewildered by the underlying excitement in his voice, Susan turned and went into the darkened shelter of the gazebo. "Why?"

"I wanted to let you know that I'm leaving tomorrow."

"Leaving? To go where?"

He laughed, his excitement pouring over. "I was notified today that the Atlanta Aces want me for their farm team. I'm to report to Florida tomorrow, which means catching the first flight out of here."

Susan sat down with a thump, her legs no longer capable of bearing her weight. "You really mean it, don't you? You're going to play professional ball?"

Tony sat down beside her, grabbing both her hands. "Yes. Now we can get married, honey, just as we planned. I'll have to find out when I can get some time off to come back to get you, but we're going to get married as soon as I can arrange it." His determined tone made her realize how serious he was.

"Oh, Tony, everything's happening so fast!" She could no longer see him, but she could feel the heat from his body radiating the male scent of aftershave that would always make her think of Tony whenever she smelled it. Unaware of her actions Susan reached for him, clutching his warm muscular body to her. "I don't want you to go," she whispered.

His arms slid around her in a possessive grip. Her hair brushed against his face and he touched his lips to her forehead. His hand slid gently under her chin and lifted it, so that his lips found hers.

It had been months since she'd seen him, lonely months of wondering how they were going to make their dreams come true. Now that she was in his arms, anything seemed possible.

His first kiss was warm and seeking, and she felt as though she were exploding in a million different pieces with the pleasure of being in his arms. He seemed to sense her total surrender and drew back for a moment, giving them both a chance to breathe. Then he began to kiss her once more.

His second kiss became more possessive and the intimate exploration of his tongue created a tremor within her she couldn't control.

By the time Tony relaxed his hold on her, Susan refused to allow him to pull completely away. Instead, her hands crept under the pullover shirt he wore and stroked across his broad chest. Her lips found the corded strength of his neck and began a trail of warm, moist kisses.

"Susan, baby, you've got to stop that," he growled into her ear. She ignored him. Her inquisitive fingers roamed to his back, where the indented spine continued to lure her into exploring. Her head fell against his shoulder, her long hair falling loose from its casual topknot and snaking down along his shoulder and arm. His mouth unerringly found hers once again.

Susan never remembered how they came to the point where they were both nude and stretched out on the cushioned bench. She could still recall her panicky feeling when she recognized what was happening. Tony's hard body pressed down against her, his leg heavy across her thighs as his hands explored her quivering body. Susan knew she had no business being there with him like that—knew she had to leave right away, but a treacherous feeling of languor and longing to enjoy for a few minutes more the strong feelings he evoked within her lured her to imitate Tony's movements. Her hands continued to stroke the muscular contours that gave mute evidence to Tony's athletic way of life.

Once his hand reached her inner thighs and began a pulsating rhythm she lost all reasoning powers. He gently nudged her legs apart with his knee as he continued to kiss her with slow mind-drugging movements of his lips and tongue. She was scarcely aware when he moved between her legs, then paused.

"Oh, honey, I'm sorry, I can't wait. I love you so much. And we'll be married in a few weeks. Let me show you my love," he whispered, his voice husky with controlled passion. "I don't want to hurt you," he murmured. She stiffened at his words, but she was too late. With strong, steady pressure he possessed her, his mouth moving on hers at the same time, absorbing any sound she might have made.

After the first sharp pain Susan discovered a very

pleasurable sensation. Her body took over and responded to his lovemaking as though instinctively aware of how to please him. It was too late for second thoughts. Besides, this was Tony. Whatever Tony did was all right.

Susan felt a tension, a continuing tightening deep within her as Tony's pace quickened. He continued to plunge deep within her and she gasped as a sudden shower of stars fell around them. Her body made a convulsive contraction that overcame Tony's control and he made one last plunge, then collapsed in her arms.

They must have slept as they lay, Tony's weight partially resting on the side of the bench. Susan felt dazed when she became aware of where she was, her arms draped around Tony, his body partially covering hers. When she attempted to move he stirred.

She heard him mutter something, his tone disgusted. She felt a frisson of fear as she realized what they had done.

"You okay?" he asked as he pulled away from her.

She nodded, then realized he couldn't see her. "Yes," she answered hesitantly.

She heard him moving, a rustle of clothes, then he placed something across her. "Here are your clothes," he whispered.

Susan automatically pulled them on, wondering what to do or say. Tony sank down beside her, pulling her back into his arms.

"I didn't mean this to happen, baby, you know that, don't you?"

Fear of rejection caused Susan to stiffen. "Do you think I did?"

He began to stroke her back, trying to remove the sudden stiffness he felt. "Oh, no, honey, that isn't what I meant. I didn't do anything to protect you."

"Oh."

They sat there in silence as Tony continued to stroke her. "I've got to leave tomorrow—I have no choice."

"Yes."

"As soon as I know where I'll be staying I'll call you, okay?"

"Okay."

"Dammit, Susan, don't make this harder for me. If I could, I'd take you with me. As it is, I'll be back to get you before you even realize I've been gone."

Although the warmth of Tony's body still protected her from the cool night air, Susan suddenly felt alone. Tony was leaving. There'd be an entire continent between them.

"I need to go inside, Tony," she murmured softly.

"I know, love, I know. I'm so sorry for losing control tonight. You don't need the extra worry."

"What do you mean?"

"Oh, Susan, don't you understand you could be pregnant? I didn't want to start our marriage out on that note."

"If I'm pregnant, I'll have to face the consequences."

"No. If you're pregnant, *we'll* face the consequences . . . together."

"It may not happen."

51

"I know."

"I don't want you to marry me because you have to."

She could feel his chest shake just as she heard his chuckle. "Believe me, Susan, I wouldn't be marrying you because I have to. You've been all I've wanted for a wife since I first met you. But six was a little young to propose." He kissed her softly on the forehead. "Why do you think I want to play professional ball? I've got to make enough money that even your mother will consider me worthy of you." He kissed her cheek softly. "Go on inside, love. Just don't forget I love you, and I'll be back to get you in just a few weeks."

Susan went back to the house that night and dreamed of Tony, confident in their love for each other. She waited for him to call, she waited for him to write, and she waited for him to come back for her, but she never heard from him again.

It was a long time before Susan finally fell asleep that night.

3

Late the next afternoon Donna, Susan's secretary, burst through her office doorway, her eyes wide with excitement. "Susan! Tony Antonelli is here to see you. Omigosh, he's even better looking in person. I didn't know you knew him. Why didn't you tell me?"

Susan had been dictating when she was interrupted and she stared at Donna in surprise. Her unflappable, experienced secretary generally had a professional air about her that could not be shaken regardless of the crisis, yet there she was blithering like a teenager over a rock star. She eyed the woman thoughtfully.

The expression on Susan's face stopped Donna in her tracks. What had she done? She'd just burst into Susan's office, that's what she'd done. Susan generally kept her door open, so that when she shut it, the closed door was a signal that she didn't want to be disturbed. Donna could feel the heat of embarrassment surge through her.

"I'm sorry for bursting in like that, Susan. You can imagine my surprise when I looked up and saw Tony Antonelli standing there, smiling at me." She noted that Susan had not changed her expression, but continued to watch her impassively.

"Did he say why he was here?" Susan asked.

"Oh, of course he did. He said he wanted to talk with you if you had a few minutes." She took in the stack of files Susan was methodically reviewing. "I didn't bother to ask if he had an appointment because I knew I would have remembered it."

Susan glanced at her watch. It was after four o'clock. She, too, studied the files on her desk, then sighed with resignation. Whatever it was he wanted to discuss with her must be very important, for she had told him how busy she would be today. The Tony she remembered would never have come to the office without very good reason. She was afraid he found Steve good reason, so she might as well get it over with.

She carefully laid the microphone down on the transcriber and stood up. "Of course I'll see him," she said with a smile that successfully hid her trepidation. She walked to the open door and paused. Tony stood in front of Donna's desk, his head bowed as though his thoughts had taken him far away from the quiet luxury of the law office. Donna slipped past Susan and returned to her desk.

"Hello, Tony."

His head snapped up and he stared at her in disbelief. The woman in the severely tailored navy suit, with her hair pulled into a knot low on her neck, bore little resemblance to the woman he'd seen the night before.

"Susan?"

She smiled. "Come in," she said, motioning him to enter.

He tried to regain lost ground, tried to remember his anger and bitter feelings toward this woman who had hidden from him for ten long years the fact that he had a son. Instead, all he could think about was the tremendous change in the woman he had known as a child. The change was not for the better. It was almost as if all her joy and excitement had been removed, leaving this calm, unemotional person instead. What had happened to her to have caused such a tremendous change? Was she still grieving for Michael?

None of his thoughts were apparent as Tony stepped past her into her office. "Very nice," he murmured, unsure of how to broach the subject now that he was there.

"Thank you."

She motioned to one of the chairs, then sat down in another one a few feet away. She wondered why Tony was so insistent on talking with her. It was obvious from the set of his jaw that he was determined to discuss something. Didn't he understand that he was eleven years late with an apology, if that was what he intended. Somehow a simple "Oops, sorry" seemed singularly inappropriate.

Her training helped Susan to control her emotional reaction to his presence, and she appeared relaxed and courteous. Her restless night showed in the slight mauve shadows under her eyes, intensifying her look of vulnerability. She wished she'd gotten more sleep the night before rather than spending so many hours reliving the painful memories that Tony's visit had evoked.

"I'm sure you won't be surprised to learn I didn't get much sleep last night." Tony's gruff words almost made her jump, they were so similar to her own thoughts. "I had to sift through some strong emotions before I could begin to deal with them." He leaned forward, resting his elbows on his knees.

"I can imagine," she said quietly.

"Can you?" He glanced up under his thick brows. "I wonder. Do you have any idea how it feels to think you know someone, and then have them act in such a way that you realize you never knew them at all?" His tone was almost meditative as he turned his head and stared out the window.

"Of course I do. That's exactly the way I felt when I realized all your talk about calling me, and arranging to marry me, were all lies. You've just described the feelings I had at that time."

"What are you talking about?" He was staring at her with a puzzled expression. "I never lied to you in my life. But how do you think I felt when I thought you felt the same way about me, while all the time you were making plans to marry Michael?"

Suddenly too agitated to sit still, Susan stood up and went over to the window. With her back to him she finally spoke. "You know better than anyone, Tony, that I never had any plans to marry Michael."

"Oh, c'mon, Susan. That's all your mother talked about for years, and you know it."

She turned and looked at him. "If you'll remember correctly, you, Michael and I spent years laughing at most of Mother's plans regarding Michael and me."

Tony stood up and walked slowly toward her. "When did the two of you stop laughing, Susan?"

She stared up at him in disbelief. Was he trying to place the blame of not knowing about Steve on her? She could feel the cold anger begin to build within her as she remembered the scared seventeen-year-old he'd so blithely forgotten on his way to becoming a star.

"I quit laughing the day I faced the fact that I was pregnant by a man who professed to love me but who disappeared out of my life when I most needed him!"

"You know, that righteous anger is a good touch, and that story may have impressed your sympathetic friends, but you seem to forget it's me who's your audience this time. And we both know I did everything *but* disappear." He watched her eyes snap. "I *am* curious, though. Did Michael ever realize Steve wasn't his?"

Her hand swung before Susan consciously recognized her reaction to his insult, but Tony's legendary quick reflexes caused him to grab her by the wrist, swaying with his whole body as he stopped her swing. "Sorry, sweetheart. I don't allow anyone to slap me, not even an illustrious Spencer-McCormick.''

Susan could not remember ever having been so angry. For the first time in her life she experienced what she'd always thought was merely an expression —she glared at him through a red haze.

Her breathing, as she took several deep, steadying breaths, was the only sound in the office When she felt she had herself under control, she said, "I don't know why you've come back, Tony, or the reason that you are in this office, but I don't intend to listen to your guilt-based accusations and insults. All right. So you didn't handle things as well eleven years ago as you would now. I can accept that." She felt her knees starting to tremble in reaction to her emotional state, and she casually seated herself in a chair by the window. "Why don't we consider your apology has been made and accepted, and leave it at that."

"My *apology!* What in the hell do I have to apologize for? Not only did you disregard everything we had planned together, not only did you decide that a McCormick was a much better risk in the marriage stakes than the housekeeper's son, but rather than let me know you were pregnant you jump at the chance to use the pregnancy to consolidate your position, and you think *I* owe *you* an apology?" His voice had risen with each phrase, and Susan found herself on her feet once more.

Her voice shaking with intensity, she started toward him. "You really are a bastard, aren't you? But don't worry, that isn't anything I just learned about you. You want to know why you never heard about

Steve? Well, I'll tell you. Because I didn't know how to get in touch with you, that's why. I waited and waited and waited for you to write. I watched the mail every day for weeks until it began to dawn on me that you had never had any intention of writing me. All those loving endearments had rolled off your tongue, and like a fool I believed you. But I paid for it. Oh, God, did I pay for it. I don't know what I would have done if Michael hadn't been there. He was the only person I trusted enough to tell. And he stuck by me. He was the one who suggested we get married and let the family think the baby was his. He knew that as far as Mother knew, he was the only one I ever dated. He didn't push me. In fact, he even offered to try to contact you himself, if that was what I wanted. But it wasn't. I had no desire to see you forced to return home and marry me. My dreams died hard, Tony, but they did die. I don't owe you any apologies for anything. You did your very best to make my life a disaster, but thank God I had Michael. He was worth ten of you!''

It was only when she stopped talking that Susan realized she was crying, the tears pouring down her cheeks in an unchecked flow. She couldn't remember the last time she had cried, but it had been years—probably not since Michael's death. Tony had managed to unleash all of her emotions and if he didn't like being the brunt of them, that was too damned bad!

Tony stood there, an arm's length from her, his face gradually softening as he continued to watch her. He reached out tentatively and brushed one of her cheeks. "You never got any of my letters, did you?"

Her laugh was a half-sob. "You never give up, do you? Does it somehow absolve you of your guilt feelings to pretend?"

He placed his hands on her shoulders and gently rocked her until she was forced to rest her hands on his chest for balance. "Oh, Susan, what have we done to each other?"

She tried to push him away, but he held on, steadily tightening the pressure until she was standing in the circle of his arms. She dropped her head wearily against his shoulder, the outburst of rage leaving her perilously weak. "It doesn't matter anymore. It was all so long ago. It could have happened to two other people."

"But it didn't. It happened to us and there is a young boy out there that shares everything we are or ever hoped to become." He tilted her chin slightly with his forefinger. "I think we need to sit down and try to work out the misunderstandings. It's important to all of us."

Susan had forgotten how it felt to be held in a man's arms. Most particularly, in Tony's arms. The strange familiarity of being back within the protection of his quiet strength was curiously peaceful, considering the storm that had recently filled the room.

"Why do you insist there was some misunderstanding? The only misunderstanding I can see is that for some reason you think I chose to marry Michael rather than to marry you."

"Are you telling me that isn't true?"

"Are you going to believe me if I tell you?"

He studied her soft features, so dear to him. "Yes, love, I'll believe you."

"The only reason Michael and I married was because I was pregnant and didn't know which way to turn. I wanted the baby"—she felt his arms tighten with her words—"and Michael understood my fear of telling Mother and giving her control over us."

"Then your mother didn't know about the pregnancy?"

"No. She has always explained to everyone that he was premature."

"How can she look at him and believe he isn't mine?"

"She never had any reason to think otherwise. Remember, she never knew I was seeing you."

"Then how did she explain away all my phone calls to you?"

She jerked back in his arms, and stared up at him. "What phone calls?"

"The ones I made when you didn't answer any of my letters."

"You really did write to me?"

"I really did."

"And you called?"

"Many times. Sometimes I talked to your housekeeper . . . Dora, was it?"

"Yes, I think Dora was working for Mother then."

"Your mother always said she had given you my message but that you had been with Michael and no doubt hadn't found the time to return my call."

"Mother said that?"

"Oh, yes. She was very civil."

"Mother? Did she know who it was?"

"Of course. I always left my name and phone number."

"Didn't you find it strange that she wasn't cold to you?"

"Your mother has always treated me with aloof politeness."

Susan was quiet for a long while. Then she spoke in a faraway voice. "Mother knew you were calling me. She must have also known you were writing, but she never mentioned it to me. Not ever."

"The last time I called, your mother informed me of your engagement to Michael and suggested it would be better if I didn't call again."

"Tony, Michael and I were never engaged. We went to Mexico and got married and came back and told everyone. We knew they would never agree to our getting married that young. I was seventeen, he was eighteen. We figured if we presented them with the accomplished fact, they would have to accept it."

"Obviously, they accepted it."

"After Mother read us her sensible, sane approach to life sermon and the sins of impetuous behavior. She insisted on a church wedding, so that no one could be cheated out of the spectacle, and Michael and I agreed to go along with it."

"When did you get married?"

"July."

"You didn't wait very long after I left, did you?" There was still a hint of bitterness in his voice.

"I knew three weeks after you left there was a very

good chance I might be pregnant. I waited another month, hoping I was wrong before I talked to Michael about it. He saw no point in our wasting any time, once we decided.''

"Why didn't you try to contact me through Mama?"

"For the same reason I decided against tracking you down and confronting you with what had happened. If you didn't care enough to contact me on your own, I knew we had nothing upon which to build any kind of relationship.''

"You still don't believe I tried to contact you, do you?"

"Yes, as a matter of fact, I do. But you have to understand that I can't change the thinking of eleven years in a few short minutes. I can see Mother doing exactly what she did. She assumed that eventually you would get tired of writing and phoning when you never received a response. When that didn't work, she made up a phony engagement.''

"The question is, what do we do about it now?"

Startled, Susan asked, "It's a little late to do anything, don't you think? It certainly wouldn't accomplish much to confront Mother after all this time.''

"Susan, I was raised without a father. I can't stand by and watch my son in the same situation without trying to do something about it.''

Susan could feel the heat flow through her at his low-voiced comment. What could he be suggesting? Trying to sound as noncommittal as possible, Susan said, "Yes, I can understand your feelings.''

"Let me get acquainted with him, spend some time with him. Let's give you and me a chance to catch up on the last few years."

"There's no reason to include me in your plans, you know. I have no objection to your seeing Steve and spending time with him. I don't believe any child can receive too much love. And you'll find him very easy to love." *He's like you in so many ways,* she thought, unaware of what she was admitting.

Tony stared at her, wondering if she had any idea how he felt. She had lived with the knowledge for years. He was just now coming to grips with the idea. She sounded so calm. Didn't she have any deep-seated feelings at all anymore?

"You're telling me you don't mind my getting to know Steve, but that's as far as it goes?" he asked.

She nodded. "Yes. Whatever you and I once shared is no longer there and I see no reason to pretend."

Tony stared at her for a long moment. "I see," he said finally. "All right. If that's the way you want it." He started for the door, then paused. "It's all right, then, if I go ahead and call Steve?"

She nodded, unable to say anything else. If he would only get out of her office before she broke down! He smiled, the flashing smile that had always made her knees weak. Obviously, that was one thing that would never change.

"Thanks for your time, counselor. I promise to stay out of your way." The door closed softly behind him.

She wondered how long it would take her to find

the concentration necessary to focus once again on her work.

Susan slowly came awake, relaxed in the knowledge that it was Saturday and she didn't need to hurry. It had been a hard week, although the dinner party the night before had gone much better than she expected.

Harry Brulanger had been quiet but amusing in a rather droll way. If he were kin to anyone besides Lorraine she might have accepted his invitation for dinner, but she knew better. Any sign of encouragement and Lorraine and her mother would be off, eagerly making wedding plans.

Her thoughts turned to her mother and how she had manipulated events eleven years ago. Susan knew she had to talk to someone about what she'd learned from Tony. She had arrived early enough at her parents' home to find her father alone for a few minutes. He'd been in his study, reading, when she peeked in the door. She stood there watching him for a moment, then tapped on the open door. He glanced up over his reading glasses and smiled. "Come in, baby. I didn't hear you come in."

She stepped inside, carefully closing the door behind her. "That's because I snuck in, Daddy. I was hoping to get a chance to talk with you."

He placed the book and his glasses down on the table next to his favorite chair. Motioning to the chair next to him, he said, "Fine. What shall we talk about?"

Her father was a slim man of medium height. His

unobtrusive style of dress once caused a younger Susan to accuse him of being able to lose himself in a crowd of two. She'd gotten her clear blue eyes and slender build from him; often she wished she could have inherited his wisdom as well.

She sat down, relaxing for the first time that day. "I need your advice, Daddy."

A slight smile lifted the corners of his mouth. "I've never been very good at giving advice, you know."

"Actually, you've always given excellent advice. The trouble has been trying to corner you so you would."

"So you think you've cornered me tonight?"

"I hope so." She hesitated, unsure of how to begin. Finally, she looked up and met his calm gaze. "Tony Antonelli is back in town." She watched for a reaction, but got none. Her father would make an excellent poker player. "You know who he is, don't you?"

His clear blue eyes held a wicked gleam. "Yes, dear, I believe as old and decrepit as I am, I still know who Tony Antonelli is, and the fact he won Most Valuable Player this year in the World Series."

"You know very well that's not what I meant!" She tried hard to mask her agitation, willing herself to sit quietly in the chair.

Stephen Spencer studied her for a moment, the gleam disappearing from his eyes. "Are you afraid he'll make trouble over Steve?" her father asked in a quiet voice.

Susan's head jerked up, her body jolted by his unexpected statement. "You know about Steve?"

His eyes narrowed as he studied the confusion in her face. "Susan, anyone looking at Steve has to be reminded of Tony at that age. He's an exact replica of him."

"Does Mother know?"

He paused. "I believe your mother has chosen not to see the resemblance."

"What am I going to do?"

"What do you want to do?"

Once again he surprised her. She hadn't thought about it that way. She had wondered what she could do, perhaps, but never what she *wanted* to do. "I don't want to see Steve hurt."

"Do you think Tony will hurt him?"

"Not intentionally, perhaps, but yes, I think having Tony in his life will be the worst thing possible for Steve. He's content now. Once he's spent time with Tony, he'll always yearn for more."

"Are you thinking of Steve . . . or yourself?"

"Me? Of course not. Anything I might have felt for Tony was over years ago."

"I wonder. You were his shadow for so many years, and you were such a loyal little thing. It's hard to believe those emotions would ever disappear."

"Well, they did." Stephen made no response and for a while they sat there together in companionable silence. Susan eventually spoke. "Did you ever know of Tony calling me, Daddy?"

"When?"

"Oh, back when he first went with the farm team."

"You mean, just before you married Michael?"

She refused to meet his gaze. "Yes."

"I really don't remember, why?"

"He said he did."

"Was it important?"

"Of course it was important! I needed to talk to him then. Desperately. Only I couldn't reach him, and I never got any calls from him. He told me yesterday that he *had* called, several times in fact, and left messages, but that I never called him back."

"Would you have married him, Susan?"

Without realizing the implications of her answer, she replied instantly, "Oh, yes!"

His eyes grew sad as her father continued to study her. At last he sighed. "Poor Michael."

Susan got up from her chair and knelt by her father. "Oh, Daddy, not you, too. Tony assumed I hadn't told Michael the truth, too." Tears welled in her eyes and she brushed them away impatiently.

"That wasn't what I meant, dear. Of course Michael knew Tony was the father. I was just remembering how often he lied to help you and Tony, even to accepting Tony's baby as his own. He was quite a man."

Susan rested her head on her father's knee and nodded. "Yes, he was," she responded in a muffled voice. "I really did love him, and I tried my best to make him happy."

Her father stroked her hair as she knelt there. "I'm glad to know that. He deserved your love."

He continued to stroke her head until she finally raised it. "What should I do about Tony, Daddy?"

He shook his head. "I can't tell you that, I'm

afraid. You're the only one who can make that decision."

As she got up from her kneeling position, she tried for flippancy. "Too bad I can't be more like Mother. She has no trouble making all kinds of decisions for other people."

Her father reached for her hand and patted it. "Don't be too hard on your mother, Susan," he said, and stood up. "She has had a difficult time with life. It's unfortunate that none of the people she loved ever measured up to her expectations. It's been her affliction that she's been unable to accept us as we are. Instead, she's tried to make us what she wants us to be."

"How can you bear it, Daddy? I've often wondered how you've managed to live with her all these years."

He pulled her close to his side, hugging her. "I love your mother very much, Susan. I always have, and I always will. I've been able to accept her as she is. Maybe someday you'll be able to do the same."

"Oh, Daddy, I don't know. How can I ever forgive her for interfering in my life? I would have married Tony years ago and none of this would be facing me now."

"True. Are you wishing away those years you had with Michael, making a mockery of what he did for you and Steve?"

She looked at him in horror. "No!"

"Since you can't change the past, Susan, it might be a good idea for you to accept it and put it behind you." He opened the door and went into the hallway. "We'd better let your mother know you're here. You know how she frets about things."

The doorbell interrupted Susan's thoughts and she glanced at the clock with dismay. It was only eight o'clock. Hannah was gone for the weekend and Steve had spent the night with one of his friends rather than have Susan pick him up after last night's dinner party. She would have to go to the door herself.

It rang again as she dashed down the hall, pulling on her robe as she ran. Breathless, she called, "Who is it?" and quickly tied the sash.

"Tony."

No, it couldn't be. She wasn't ready for him, not first thing in the morning. She opened the door.

"Good morning." He stood there grinning, looking incredibly virile in a crimson pullover shirt and fleece-lined denim jacket, his jeans outlining his well-developed thighs.

She stepped back with a sigh. "Good morning, Tony. You might as well come in."

"Such an enthusiastic greeting. I'm overcome."

"Steve isn't here."

One brow rose as he took in her attire. "And you were sleeping in?"

"Something like that."

"I'm sorry I woke you."

"Oh, I was awake, just not out of bed." She turned and started back down the hall. "Come on back and I'll put on some coffee." She filled the pot with water and carefully poured it into the machine, then flipped on the switch. When she turned around, she saw Tony leaning against the counter watching her with amused interest.

"Aren't your feet cold?" he asked. She glanced down at her bare toes peeking from below her robe.

"As a matter of fact, they are. I'll get some clothes on and be back in a moment." She indicated the coffee machine. "Help yourself when it's done."

She tried to keep her mind free of all thought while she dressed. She had agreed that Tony could get to know Steve, but she wasn't at all sure how she was going to handle seeing him on a regular basis.

When she returned to the kitchen in jeans and a long-sleeved plaid shirt, her feet shod warmly in socks and sneakers, she found Tony sitting at the table, calmly reading the paper and sipping a cup of coffee.

He glanced up. "I happened to see your paper outside when I came up. Hope you don't mind my getting it."

She shrugged. "Not at all." She poured herself a cup of coffee and sat down across from him. He laid the paper aside and once again watched her, which made her nervous.

"Are you having second thoughts about letting me spend time with Steve?" His voice showed little inflection and his face gave nothing of his thoughts away.

She sighed, recalling her conversation with her father. "No, not really."

He grinned. "Good."

"But I have wondered what sort of relationship you're hoping to build with him."

"How about friendship?"

"How many ten-year-old friends do you have?"

"Several, why?"

She was certain her surprise registered on her face. Of course, he was a famous ballplayer. They would naturally flock around him. "How long do you intend to stay in Santa Barbara?"

"Permanently."

"You mean you've quit baseball?"

"Not necessarily, but during the off season I intend to stay here. I'm looking for a place to buy now, which is one of the reasons I'm here. I thought maybe you and Steve would like to come with me today. I'm going to be looking at some property along the coast. Hopefully, I'll find something I like. I'm sick of hotel rooms."

She'd just started to say, "I'm not sure when Steve—" when she heard the front door slam.

"Mom! There's the neatest car parked out front," he hollered as he trotted down the hall. "It's silver and—" He came to an abrupt halt. "Tony! Is that your car?"

"Sure is. I take it you like it."

"Wow, do I ever. Is there a chance I could maybe go for a ride in it?"

"Funny you should ask. I was just asking your mother if you two might want to take a drive along the coast with me today while I look at some property."

Steve's eyes widened and his infectious grin appeared. "Hey, that would be great, wouldn't it, Mom?" He bounced over to the table. "You wanna go?" There was no doubt in Susan's mind about Steve's preference.

"Sure. Sounds like fun," she lied. She was rewarded by an exuberant hug.

"I've gotta call Scotty and tell him I can't meet him to play ball this morning," he said as he dashed out of the kitchen once more.

"Such enthusiasm," Susan muttered.

"Such energy," Tony added.

"That, too. You may not be aware of what you're getting yourself into." For the first time since he'd seen her last Wednesday, Tony received a relaxed, natural smile from Susan. His heart lurched in his chest. It was so much like the young girl he'd once known. Was there any other trace of her in this composed woman? He was going to do his damnedest to find out.

Susan offered to sit in the backseat, which was truly a sacrifice of the highest order, since there was no room in the back area for such things as knees and legs. Tony explained that Steve could sit in the smaller space more comfortably, a fact neither of them could argue, and Susan resigned herself to spending the day next to Tony.

With Steve's enthusiasm for the venture, and the hundred and one questions he had for Tony, Susan didn't have to worry about making conversation. She was literally along for the ride. It was just as well. Spending the day with Tony wasn't the smartest decision she'd ever made. It gave her too much time to compare her past to her present. Although maturity had made certain changes about him, Susan recognized many familiar mannerisms, such as the way he tilted his head when he talked to her, the rumbling baritone of his voice that managed to touch an inner spark every time she heard it and the way his eyes flashed with good humor. When he grinned she was instantly reminded of the boy in the backseat, who shared the same wide smile. How could she ever have forgotten?

By the end of the day she grudgingly had to admit that Tony had his full share of charisma. Steve was totally enthralled, and if she were honest, she had to admit he'd woven something of a spell around her as well.

They stopped for hamburgers and shakes before going home. Two of the places they'd seen had caught Tony's imagination and he began to ply Susan with questions as to her choice between the two. She refused to give him a definitive answer. Instead, she agreed with him when he pointed out their good qualities and possible drawbacks.

By the time they returned home, Steve needed no prodding to get ready for bed. Out of politeness Susan invited Tony in, hoping he'd say no. He didn't.

"Would you like something to drink?" she asked as she stood in the middle of the living room.

"No, thanks." He came toward her in a steady stride. "Thank you for today, Susan. It meant a great deal to me." He stopped in front of her.

She tried to control her reaction to his closeness by

refusing to step back from him. "Steve had a great time, as I'm sure you could tell."

Tony slipped his hand under Susan's chin, raising it slightly. "And how about Steve's mother? Did she have a great time, too?"

It wasn't fair that he should have such an effect on her. Her heart fluttered like a bird's wings in her chest, and she was having trouble with her breathing. Susan tried to find her voice. "I, uh, enjoyed today, too, Tony. Thank you." She glanced up at him, then wished she hadn't. The smoldering message in his eyes did nothing to help her pulse rate.

His arms slid around her waist and he lowered his lips to hers. There had been many women in his arms during the past eleven years, so why did it feel so natural and right to have Susan there once more? Tony took possession of her as though she'd always been his. His mouth began a gentle exploration and he felt the tenseness leave her body.

She didn't want to feel anything for him, but she could no longer deny that she had a strong attraction to this man. Susan relaxed in his arms, her mouth responding to his, her body conscious of his as she leaned into him.

"Uh, Mom, could I have some ice cream before I go to bed?"

Susan and Tony sprang apart as though they'd received an electric shock. Steve stood before them in his pajamas, his hands resting lightly on his hips. Although his face was flushed, his eyes danced with amusement. "I think maybe you guys need a chaperon or something."

Tony burst out laughing. Susan was mortified. She had not dated since Michael's death, so Steve had never seen her with another man. How could he seem so unconcerned? Surely he should be jealous, or at the very least resentful. On the contrary, he appeared delighted.

With commendable composure under the circumstances, Susan nodded. "I guess a small bowl won't hurt. We can't have you dying of starvation before morning."

When Steve disappeared into the kitchen, Tony chuckled. "It doesn't look like we shocked Steve by necking in the living room, does it?"

Susan could feel the color flush her cheeks and attempted to change the subject. "I really need to get some sleep as well. It's been a rather long day."

He grinned. "Yes, hasn't it? However, it's good to see some color in your face. If nothing else, the day did that for you."

If you only knew, she thought. "Yes, well, thank you again for inviting us."

"And here's your hat, don't let me rush you off," he added. She followed him to the door. He turned the knob, then glanced down at her. "I don't know what else Michael taught you, Susan, but he certainly managed to teach you to kiss!" The door opened and he left, closing it gently behind him.

"Ooohhhhh!" How dare he! Susan stormed down the hallway to her bedroom, wishing she had something to throw.

As Tony drove away, his thoughts were on the two people he'd just left. He'd been kidding himself when he'd decided he had no feelings for Susan. She'd been so much a part of his life that unbeknownst to him, he'd carried her with him in his heart all these years. Not that he intended to admit that to her. He could see that as far as she was concerned, her present life was all she needed or wanted. She had her home, her career, and her son. What more could she want?

Tony knew he would have to take it one step at a time. Steve was so lovable, it hadn't taken him long to wrap himself around Tony's heartstrings, right there next to his mother. She and Michael had done a fine job with him. He prayed to God he'd be given the opportunity to pick up where Michael had been forced to leave off.

"If you can hear me, Michael, I want you to know that I'll love them, and be there for them, if I'm given the chance."

Once again he saw the picture of the three of them on the mantel, and he saw the gently smiling gray eyes gazing at him. Michael had loved them, too. *Will I be given that chance?*

4

~~~~~~~~~~~~~~~~~~~

The inviting aroma of freshly brewed coffee wafted its way into Susan's restful sleep. She stretched and slowly opened her eyes. The kitten calendar hanging next to the bed caught her attention. The tiny feline star of the month warily eyed a young turkey, which was just as warily returning the stare.

November. Tony had been back a month. She rolled over and buried her head under her pillow. Nothing had been the same since he exploded into their lives.

Steve was already growing used to having him around. He still talked about the hiking trip and the fun they'd had—and how excited everyone had been to have Tony join them. Susan had had to smile and appear pleased with each telling. Damn the man anyway! She had done her best to avoid him, and had been fairly successful, but she still had to listen to Steve rave on and on about him, ad nauseum.

A sudden thought occurred to her and she bolted upright in the bed. *I'm jealous! I'm actually jealous of the close relationship forming between the two of them!* She stared off in space, thinking furiously. *How humiliating!* She threw off her covers and got out of bed, then forced herself to look in the mirror. *Aren't you ashamed? Steve is happier than he's ever been, and you're petty enough to resent the fact it wasn't you who accomplished that fact.* She shook her head sadly. *I thought better of you. I really did.*

Another strong whiff of coffee caught her attention. *There's nothing like a cup of fresh coffee to console you when you're busy discovering your character defects,* she pointed out to herself. She picked up her hairbrush and vigorously ran it through her hair.

Since it was Saturday and she had nothing planned, Susan decided to be lazy, so she picked up her robe lying at the end of the bed and slipped her arms through its full, flowing sleeves. *Coffee first, then you can get dressed.*

After a quick stop in the bathroom to wash her face and try to get awake, she started down the hallway to the kitchen.

She heard Steve talking to Hannah and smiled. Another sign that her young son was growing up—he now let her sleep in on weekends. She could well remember the times when he'd be bouncing on her bed at dawn, reminding her the day had begun. *He's growing up so fast!* she lamented. *Where had the last ten years gone?*

When she reached the kitchen door Susan discovered it wasn't Hannah Steve was talking to with such animation. Tony sat at the small kitchen table, his long, muscular legs thrust out in a relaxed position, crossed at the ankles. He registered her shock at finding him in her kitchen and slowly smiled.

"Good morning," he said, his eyes twinkling.

The bright gold of his pullover sweater emphasized his broad shoulders and powerful arms. Susan was uncomfortably aware of how little she wore. She nervously tugged at the neck of her robe. "I'm sorry. I didn't know you were here," she muttered, and backed out of the kitchen.

Tony came to his feet in a graceful lunge. "Don't leave; you look fine. Coffee's made. Wouldn't you like a cup?"

How had he managed to reach her side so quickly? She could smell his aftershave, and was almost close enough to touch him. Her fingers trembled at the thought. *This is crazy! I used to act like this around him when we were teenagers! What's wrong with me?*

Tony took her hand and gently led her to the table, guiding her into the chair across from his, then reached for the coffeepot near his elbow. He poured her some and set it in front of her.

"Mom, Tony wants us to go with him this morning over to his new place. He just got the keys last night."

Susan freely admitted that mornings were not her best time, but this morning seemed to be breaking all records. She wasn't ready for Tony's presence at the moment. She admitted to herself she probably wouldn't have been ready at three in the afternoon, either, but at least she'd have had herself in some semblance of working order.

She sipped her coffee, trying to think rationally. She had agreed that Tony should get to know Steve, but she was certain she'd made it clear their plans were not to include her. So why was she being pushed into spending time with him?

Her gaze slowly focused on Tony. Was that sympathy she saw lurking in the black eyes staring at her so intently? She straightened her spine and frowned slightly. She certainly didn't need his sympathy, nor his blasted understanding.

Steve was too excited to sit still. He had been up and down from his chair several times since she'd walked into the room. Now he leaned against the table, watching her. The two sets of eyes staring at her, waiting for her response, were too much.

"I'm not going to be able to go, Steve," she muttered. "But I'm sure the two of you will have a good time."

"But Mom! You *have* to go. Tony and I don't know anything about kitchens and stuff like that. He said you'd be able to tell us what we need to buy."

She stared at the innocent face of the conniving man across from her. "Oh, did he?"

Unaware of the undercurrents, Steve agreed happily. "Yep. He said there were some things a man had to acknowledge that women knew better."

"How wise of Tony," Susan said through clenched teeth, then took another sip of her coffee.

It didn't help when Tony started to laugh. His laugh had always been one of the most attractive things about him. And it had always been impossible for Susan to ignore him in that mood. She took in the laugh lines that had formed around his eyes and the curves that accented the dimples in his cheeks. He had always hated those dimples, yet now they added to the character in his face.

"You need some breakfast, don't you?" she asked Steve.

His face broke into a grin that matched the one on the man across from her. "Oh, Mom. I ate hours ago. We've just been waiting for you to wake up so we can go."

"Well, you'll just have to wait for a while longer. I am not awake. It may take hours for me to reach that state of mind. In the meantime, I, for one, haven't had breakfast." She glanced at Tony. "How about you?"

"As a matter of fact, I ate before I came over."

She shrugged. She might as well give in as gracefully as possible. "All right. I'll eat, then I'll go get dressed so we can go."

Susan had forgotten how contagious Tony's exuberance was. By the end of the day she was windblown and tired, but exhilarated. She couldn't remember the last time she'd laughed so hard. It had almost been as though she'd forgotten how.

She stepped out of the shower that evening and caught a glimpse of herself in the oversize mirror in her bathroom. Gone was the composed, pale corporate attorney. In her place stood a flushed and admittedly glowing young woman with sparkling eyes. Tony had always had that effect on her. In that respect, nothing had changed.

Bright pictures of the day flashed through her mind—sitting in the small sports car next to Tony, with Steve curled into the poor excuse of a back seat; being aware of Tony's movements as he shifted gears, the muscles flexing in his thigh so close to her own; Tony making a game of inspecting the house and asking her advice.

They had spent the day as a family, and it had unnerved her. Tony's image was one of a confirmed bachelor. His romantic exploits had been as widely reported as his action on the diamond. Not that Susan had paid much attention, but it was hard to ignore it when his love life sometimes hit the sports segment of the six o'clock news. If Tony hadn't married by now, the obvious conclusion was he had no intention of marrying. Perhaps that was why he was so taken with Steve. He had found a son without the tedium of a marriage to produce him!

Susan blew her hair dry until it fell in disciplined waves down her back. Tony had convinced her not to wear it up today, so it had taken a beating. She wished he didn't have quite so much influence over her, but it had been obvious right from the start of the day with their early morning encounter that there was little Tony Antonelli would suggest that she could refuse.

In fact, the day had taken her back to her childhood, with Steve taking Michael's place, the two of them following Tony's lead. She'd watched Steve as he'd unconsciously mimicked Tony's walk and gestures.

Oh, Steve. None of what happened was meant to deprive you of your father. But how can I tell you that the man you idolize walked away and didn't come back when I needed him the most?

Susan stepped into the bedroom and began looking through her closet. Tony had promised to take them out to eat at one of Steve's favorite restaurants overlooking the Pacific Ocean. Knowing the futility of trying to be excluded, Susan had only insisted she needed to get cleaned up and change clothes. She glanced at her watch. Steve was no doubt impatiently waiting for her.

He wasn't. When Susan walked into the living room, Tony was alone. "Where's Steve?"

Tony stared at her with obvious approval. Once again she'd left her hair down. "Oh," he answered in a casual tone, "he decided he was too tired to go out, so he fixed himself a sandwich and went on to bed."

Susan stared at him in amazement. "Steve is in bed? At seven-thirty?"

Tony grinned at the tone of her voice. "Yes. I was surprised myself. I reminded him that he was the one who had picked out the restaurant, but he said he'd go some other time."

Susan spun on her heel and hurried down the hall. He was sick! When had it come on him? He'd seemed fine all day. She felt herself beginning to panic and sought a calm expression as she tapped on his door.

"Come in," came a sleepy voice.

She opened the door and found the room dark. Flipping on the bedside lamp, she sat down on Steve's bed. "What's wrong, Steve?" she asked softly, her hand automatically reaching for his forehead. It felt reassuringly cool.

"Nothing. I'm just tired," he muttered, his eyes refusing to meet hers.

"That's not like you to get so tired you can't eat!"

"I ate! I just decided I didn't want to go out to eat." His eyes glanced at her, then looked quickly away.

"All right. Then I'll explain to Tony that maybe we can make it some other time."

"NO!" Steve shot up off his pillow and stared at her in dismay. "I mean, why don't you and Tony go ahead and have dinner together. Hannah's here if I need anything. I'll just get some rest tonight."

She stared at her son, suddenly suspicious of his motives. "You want Tony and me to have dinner together?"

Relaxing back on his pillow, Steve gave her a smile that would melt anyone's heart. "Yeah, I thought you might like that."

"Why would you think that?"

He shrugged, a nonchalant gesture that caught her off guard with its sudden glimpse of the adult Steve would someday become. "Well, you guys are such good friends and everything. So I thought you might want to spend some time together. You know, catch up on old times and all."

"I see." Unfortunately, she certainly did see. "Tony and I have no reason to catch up on old times any more than we've already done. But it was a nice thought, Steve."

The disappointment on his face was almost her undoing. "You mean you won't go out with him?"

She shook her head gently. "I'm not interested in getting involved with anyone, Steve. You and I've talked about that before, remember?"

"But I thought Tony would be different."

"Why?"

"Because you've known him for so long."

"Which is exactly why I don't want to get involved with him. I've known him too long and too well. You know Tony has lots of women friends. I don't want to be one of them."

Those black eyes stared at her with hurt and disappointment, and she forced herself to return his gaze with calm resolution. Steve no doubt missed Michael, just as she did. He was obviously enthralled with having Tony suddenly appear in his life and show so much interest in him, but she refused to allow him to build up hopes that could never bear fruit.

"Are you still sleepy?" she asked with a soft smile.

He grinned sheepishly. "Not really. But now that I'm here I might as well go to sleep."

Susan started laughing and he reluctantly joined her. "A little extra sleep never hurt anybody, you know," she said. She leaned over and kissed him, then turned out the light and left the room, closing the door behind her.

As she walked back into the living room, she tried to decide what to tell Tony. It wouldn't do to admit that Steve was trying to play matchmaker. Nor would it do to admit how the thought had completely unnerved her.

Tony stood when she entered the room. "Is he all right?" The concern in his voice touched a response deep within her. His sincerity caused a twinge and she knew she couldn't lie.

"He's fine," she admitted. "I'm very much afraid he thought it was a good idea to give us some time alone together."

She wasn't prepared for the gust of laughter from Tony. "He must be a mind reader. Those have been my exact thoughts for the past hour or so." He strolled over to her. "I didn't get a chance to tell you how beautiful you look. Did you remember that peach was my favorite color on you?" His eyes were as bright as a starlit midnight sky.

She glanced down to look at what she was wearing. The soft, flowing dress had seemed to jump out at her when she'd gone through her closet. Had its choice been intentional? At this point she wasn't sure of anything except that Tony was standing entirely too close.

His arms slipped around her waist and pulled her unresisting body to him. "I think you've been out-voted, don't you? Doesn't the majority still rule?" he murmured, reminding her of their childhood agreement. Then all thought seemed to disappear when Tony lifted her chin with gentle fingers and brushed his lips softly against hers. As though savoring the taste, he touched her again, this time with more pressure, until her lips parted without volition.

She didn't remember sliding her arms around his neck, nor was she aware when he pulled her even closer to his body as their kiss deepened. His kisses had always had the ability to melt her, and age and experience had only added to his expertise.

He slackened his hold slightly, his lips charting a path, kiss by tiny kiss, from her mouth to the curve of her jaw. "Oh, God, Susan, if you only knew the many nights I dreamed you were in my arms, only to wake up and remember that you were no longer mine."

His words brought Susan out of the trance his kiss had placed her in. Abruptly she moved away from him. "You don't have to say things like that to me, Tony. I certainly don't believe that you've been pining away for me all these years."

"You're damn right I haven't. You taught me a lesson early in life. You were the only woman I ever wanted to marry, only I wasn't good enough for you. It was a hard lesson, but I learned it well."

"You still believe I preferred marriage to Michael, don't you? Even after what I told you?"

"You could have contacted me if you'd wanted to badly enough. And Michael was so convenient!"

The bitterness in his voice and the hurt in his eyes made her realize that Tony had not walked away unscathed from their relationship. She had never intended to discuss her marriage to Michael with anyone, particularly not Tony. But Michael was no longer there, and he had loved Tony enough not to want to see him in pain.

"You and Steve win, Tony. I'll go to dinner with you. I guess there are a few things I need to share with you, and I'll do it better after I've had a glass of wine." She smiled, hoping he would accept the peace offering.

Amazingly enough, he did. He slipped the shawl she'd laid on the arm of a chair around her shoulders and escorted her out to the car.

Their table was next to a large window overlooking the beach. Spotlights highlighted the waves rolling in, creating an ever-changing, yet never-changing view of the Pacific. A candle surrounded by a pink globe cast a warm glow of color, enclosing the two of them in a private circle of shared memories.

Susan took another sip of her wine and waited for Tony to absorb the information she had just given him. It wasn't surprising that he was stunned. Nothing in his knowledge or experience would help him to understand the type of relationship she and Michael had shared.

The light was very flattering to Tony, with his dark

coloring and flashing smile. Only he hadn't smiled much since they had sat down. Now she watched his profile as he gazed out the window abstractedly, his hand turning his wineglass in absentminded circles. He turned back to the glass, picked it up, then quickly swallowed the remaining liquid.

"I don't believe it," he finally said in a flat tone.

Whatever reaction she'd expected, that wasn't it. She wasn't used to being called a liar. How ironic. When she'd finally found the courage to share the intimate details of her marriage with someone, he didn't believe it. She shook her head wearily. Not that it mattered, really, what Tony believed.

"How could any man live with you for that many years and not make love to you, Susan?"

His agonized tone of voice surprised her. He almost sounded tortured. "Does it matter?"

"Of course it matters. I loved you. I thought you loved me, but you married someone else. Now you tell me you lived with him but didn't share a bed with him?"

"Yes."

"Why?"

She didn't want to answer his question, but she'd come this far—she really had no choice. "Because I was in love with you and Michael knew it. Michael was the brother I never had. How could I let my brother make love to me?"

"Dammit, Susan, you can't be that naive. I'm sure Michael gave you time to adjust to marriage, but no man could live with you without wanting to make love to you."

"Tony, that's what I've been trying to tell you. Michael was not attracted to me. I don't think he was ever sexually attracted to anyone."

Tony stared at her, shocked. "Are you trying to tell me that Michael was—"

"No. He wasn't interested in men, either, Tony. He just wasn't interested in a physical relationship of any kind. It was as though all his senses were caught up in making music. Didn't you ever notice that about him?"

The slight frown across his forehead was so familiar. That was the expression both he and Steve wore when they were concentrating on solving something. This time it was the mystery of Michael. Finally, he admitted, "I guess maybe I did, but never gave it any thought." He reached over and took her hand. "Were you ever able to talk to him about it?"

"Not at first. I was just grateful he seemed uninterested in me in that way. At first I was pregnant and upset. Then I got involved with school, had Steve, and continued with my schooling while Michael continued to be in his musical world." She glanced up and smiled. "Not that he ignored us. He seemed to enjoy the diversion of a wife and son, but I knew that was all we were to him." She touched his hand lightly with her finger. "Believe it or not, that was enough for me. I had had all I wanted of passion and turmoil. I relished the peaceful existence he gave us."

Tony stared at the young woman across from him. The candlelight lent a soft flush to her pale face, her hair framing her features. She was serious. Somehow she'd managed to discard the warm, passionate creature he had known and loved. What had he and Michael done to the vibrant girl-child they had grown up with?

"For a woman who has discarded any feelings of passion, that was a rather good imitation you gave to the kiss we shared earlier." His statement was deliberately provocative and he was delighted to note the deepening flush on her cheeks. She wasn't quite as cold and calculated as she would like to believe, which certainly gave him hope.

From everything he had learned after meeting her again, he knew this woman was his. He'd made his claim on her eleven years ago. She had borne his son, and he now knew that she'd never been with another man. He was determined to win her love and her trust all over again, no matter how long it took him. Steve's reaction tonight gave him his greatest encouragement. Susan might not realize it, but from now on she was going to find herself subtly and deliberately led into the trap of his arms. Only this time he had every intention of tying her to him permanently.

Tony was quiet on their way home and Susan felt she understood why. She had probably made a mistake by revealing to him the nature of her relationship with Michael. But it was too late now to do anything about it.

She wasn't sure what to say when they arrived

home. Should she invite him in or make her escape? *Where is all of your self-confidence when you need it?*

Tony gently removed the keys from her hand, opened her door, snapped on the hall light and held the door open for her. When she walked in she turned around and found him leaning against the closed front door.

"I, uh . . ." was as far as she got when he stepped forward and pulled her into his arms. The kiss he gave her was possessive, full of fire and passion. Susan gave herself up to the moment, no longer willing to be sane and sensible. This was Tony. When he finally loosened his hold, they both were having difficulty breathing. Tony reached behind him and opened the door, then gave her a mock salute.

"I'll be in touch," he said with a small smile. Then he was gone.

Susan stood there, staring at the closed door. What had all of that meant? What did she want it to mean? She wasn't sure, but she was very much afraid she was already more involved with him than she'd ever intended.

5

The oncoming headlights were nearly blinding and Susan's headache seemed to worsen with each mile. Why had she ever agreed to allow Steve to spend the day with Tony? She shook her head wearily, knowing that after she reached Tony's beach home on the coast several miles north of Santa Barbara, she'd still have to face the long drive home.

Steve had been eager to spend the time with Tony, which wasn't surprising. Christmas holidays were nearing their end and he was bored. Of course, he still enjoyed being with Tony more than anything else.

A sharp twinge of jealousy hit her. *Stop it!* she warned herself. *You've had the past three months to get used to the idea that Tony is becoming a large part of your son's life. And it's been good for him.*

Susan was intelligent enough to recognize that she couldn't be all things to Steve, but she was honest enough to acknowledge that she had wanted to be. She hadn't wanted him to need anyone else. She had wanted him to be content with their life together.

Was this what happened between divorced parents—this pain of feeling inadequate, of wanting to be needed and appreciated, and loved best of all?

Tony had been good for Steve. She'd been amazed at how in tune the two of them seemed to be. She had already noticed, even before they'd spent much time together, how many of Steve's mannerisms were similar to Tony's. It was almost as though she had passed very little of her own traits on to her son.

Stop it! she repeated determinedly, and forcefully turned her thoughts to the meeting she had just left. One of the companies she represented had held their board of directors meeting at her firm and she had spent weeks preparing for it. The chairman had expected trouble and he hadn't been wrong, but he had never lost control of the situation. She had watched with silent admiration as he handled the dissenters with serenity and dispatch.

She enjoyed her work—the calm, disciplined, formal practice that went into being a corporate attorney. She had to be constantly on top of the rapidly changing tax laws in order to keep her clients fully informed and protected. It was exciting in its own way, but today had been exhausting.

Peering at the digital clock in the dashboard of her car, she groaned. It couldn't be that late! She blinked and looked again. 10:54. Steve would be asleep by now, no doubt having given up on her. Tony would be irritated that she hadn't called to say she'd be late. To be honest, all she had thought about was getting away from the tense, highly charged arena of big business.

Susan slowed as she came to the turnoff leading to Tony's home. It was a beautiful place, but that wasn't surprising. Tony hadn't been concerned, evidently, about the amount he paid for the house, and his southern California home would answer anyone's dream of a modern palace, Susan mused.

The curving road continued to climb and she pictured the redwood and glass home perched on a cliff overlooking the ocean. She had purposely spent very little time there. How easy it would be to be lured into becoming a part of Tony's life once more, but it wasn't worth the pain.

Not that both Tony and Steve hadn't tried. They were always dreaming up some plan or activity that would include her. She had learned her lesson, though, when she discovered she wasn't immune to Tony's brand of charm. The best way to deal with it was not to deal with it, so she had been firm in refusing their many invitations to join them. *I am perfectly happy with my life now. I certainly don't need the complications of a man in it, especially Tony!*

She turned into the driveway, following its long, curving surface until it ended before a large garage. A light mist coated the windshield and she realized the wind was growing stronger. She stepped out of her car, shoved the door closed and trotted up the long stairway to the front entrance.

The door opened at the top, soft light spilling out on the deck as a large shadow filled the doorway. She glanced up and saw Tony waiting for her, a gentle smile on his face.

"What are you doing out here? You're getting wet."

"So are you."

She laughed at his reasonable tone. "You're right."

He took her arm and escorted her into the house. "I have a fire waiting for you." He slipped her coat from her shoulders, his hands lingering slightly longer than necessary. "How about a drink?"

"That sounds great, but make it a small one. I seemed to have skipped a couple of meals today, and I still have quite a drive ahead of me." She crossed over to the fireplace located in the conversation pit of the large room, its west wall was made entirely of glass. Now that they were away from the hallway, Susan discovered the only light came from the fireplace and a couple of candles placed strategically by the sofa.

She raised her voice so that he could hear her from the kitchen. "Did I by chance interrupt something? This looks like a very romantic setting you have here." She glanced around when she heard his steps, then stared in surprise. He held a tray with a small glass of wine and a large bowl of what looked to be a mouthwatering Italian stew that his mother used to make. Several large slices of French bread were on the side, lightly toasted with melted butter, causing Susan's stomach to gurgle in anticipation.

He placed the tray on the small table in front of the sofa. "Have a seat and indulge yourself. I'm afraid Steve and I ate some time ago. I was about ready to send out the troops to look for you."

She could hear no accusation in his tone but she couldn't help feeling defensive. "I'm sorry I was so late getting here. The meeting ran on longer than anyone had anticipated." She picked up a slice of the bread and took a bite. It was delicious. "What troops?" she asked with interest.

"Boy Scout, what else?"

"Ah, yes. You're getting rather involved with that group, aren't you?"

"You might say that. Steve always seems to be volunteering me for something or other these days."

"And you love it."

"How'd you guess?" His dark eyes danced, and Susan felt the sharp jab of awareness that continued to keep pace with her whenever Tony was in the vicinity. "We had quite a bit to do today. You may recall we're trying to get his model race car finished before the next scout meeting, when we're to race them. We spent a large part of the afternoon and evening working on that in the garage." He grinned, a self-satisfied smile that reminded her painfully of Steve.

She hastily picked up the glass of wine and sipped, then determinedly started on the stew. It was every bit as good as Mama Angelina's. How she missed that lady. She realized that was another tie she and Tony shared that she had conveniently placed at the back of her mind.

"You never answered my question."

He looked at her, puzzled. "I'm sorry. I must not have heard it."

"I was just commenting on the romantic mood set in here and wondered if I interrupted anything." She glanced around the room as though expecting to see a scantily clad young woman draped on a piece of furniture.

Tony grinned at her expression. "Can't you tell? I was expecting you."

Well, of course he'd been expecting her to pick up Steve, but that wasn't what she meant. From his attitude the last three months, it was clear he saw her as a childhood friend—and as Steve's mother, of course. Since the night he'd teased her about her response to his kiss he'd been polite and friendly, but nothing more—which suited her just fine.

He'd spent a great deal of time with Steve, and in general had made his presence felt. Even Hannah had gotten into the habit of quoting Tony as though he were some kind of oracle. One day Susan had said with some disgust to her, "So what you're telling me is that the gospel according to Tony says we all have to watch what sort of food we put in our bodies . . . we are what we eat, is that right?"

Hannah had the grace to blush. "I guess he's made a study of what good nutrition can do to help an athlete keep his body in top-notch condition. I found it very interesting."

"That's okay, Hannah. I didn't mean to snap. It's just that when *both* you and Steve start quoting him, I feel a little outnumbered."

For some reason she had the same feeling now, and Tony was the only other person in the room. Perhaps it was the intense way he was studying her. She continued to eat, avoiding his gaze.

"Where is Steve, by the way?"

"Asleep."

"That's not surprising. Where?"

"I went ahead and put him to bed. Told him I'd try to talk you into staying over."

His quiet words wreaked havoc within her. He made it sound so simple. She opened her mouth to protest and he held up his hands in the time-out signal. "I know you won't be working tomorrow. Hannah will be gone for the weekend, and we still have quite a bit of work to do on the race car. We have much more room to work here in my garage, and it wouldn't hurt for you to relax and do nothing for a while, would it?"

"That isn't the point."

"Then why don't you explain it to me?"

She paused, trying to marshal her arguments as well as calm her inner agitation before it showed. "We don't have any clothes here. There's no reason why I can't just bring him back tomorrow."

He grinned. "At the risk of being thought devious, I asked Hannah to pack some things for you. Your overnight case is in one of the *spare* bedrooms."

"You *are* devious, Tony, but tonight I'm too tired to care." Susan reached down and slipped off her shoes, then leaned her head back on the sofa. She closed her eyes, rubbing them distractedly.

"Are your eyes bothering you?"

"A bit. I managed to pick up a headache somewhere along the way today." It felt so good to relax, to know there would be no more demands made on her tonight.

"What did you think of supper? Steve and I made it."

"It was delicious. Mama Angelina would have been proud of you. You two make a great team."

"I think so."

She could think of nothing to say in reply. His voice had lost its teasing note, and the serious tone touched a chord deep within her. Finally, she sat up. "I believe I'll go on to bed after I've cleaned these up for you." She reached for the tray, but he stopped her.

"Leave them and go to bed, Susan. You're exhausted."

Mentally agreeing with his assessment of her condition, she wandered down the hallway, spotting her overnight case sitting at the end of the bed in one of the bedrooms. She found her nightshirt and made quick work of removing her makeup and brushing her teeth, then fell into bed.

She was unaware of Tony when he came in later to check on her. He stood near the bed, noting the circles under her eyes, her fragility, and wished he knew how to stop her from pushing herself so hard.

He'd gone slow with her over the past several weeks, getting her used to his being around. He'd made great strides with Steve, and had been the recipient of several confidences that convinced him more than ever that both of them needed him.

Tony's gaze traced the slight outline in bed and he sighed. God knew he needed both of them as well. The question was, how did he go about winning them over to his way of thinking? He retraced his steps, gently closing the door behind him. He wondered what Susan was trying to prove. Was her career so important to her, or was it what the career represented? She'd become a mother before she was little more than a child herself, accepting the responsibilities of adulthood. When would she learn that it was all right to relax and enjoy life a little? He hoped he could help her to do that. He had so much he wanted to give to her, to share with her, if she would only accept him.

Susan stirred, reluctant to give up the sleepy warmth that had enfolded her for the past several hours. She stretched, then went limp, her eyes refusing to open.

"Good morning." The husky baritone caused her lids to pop open in surprise. Susan had forgotten she had gone to bed at Tony's the night before. She certainly hadn't expected to be greeted by that voice first thing. It wasn't fair that he should look so good this early in the morning. His black curls were still damp from the shower and the beige pullover turtleneck sweater clung to his muscular chest almost indecently.

"Good morning," she parroted, not awake enough to think of anything more original to say.

"Breakfast is almost ready. Do you plan to join us?" His smile affected her as strongly as it always had. That smile had lured her into following him into several mischief-laden adventures. She would like to think she was immune to it. However, she had serious doubts about her resistance where Tony was concerned.

She sat up, the covers obligingly displaying her sleeping attire designed to look like a man's old-fashioned nightshirt, with vertical red and white stripes.

His smile widened into a grin. "It's hard for me to picture you as a sober, staid attorney in that outfit."

She glanced down, unconcerned. "That's all right. None of my clients ever see me this way."

"I should certainly hope not."

"Tony, as soon as you leave, I'll get up," she pointed out in a patient voice.

"Oh. I thought you'd let me see the rest of that dazzling piece of sleepwear."

"No."

"Too bad." He shrugged, then turned away. He looked over his shoulder when he reached the door. "Someday, maybe?" he said hopefully.

She shook her head firmly. The look of disappointment was very well done if he'd been able to control the dancing light in his eyes. "Good-bye, Tony," she insisted.

He laughed, closing the door behind him.

Susan stood up, glancing down at the brief length of her shirt. It modestly reached mid-thigh, but curved to her hips on each side. She entered the adjoining bathroom, slid the shirt over her head and stepped into the shower.

She wished she knew what Tony was up to by insisting they stay the night. She remembered the boy too well to believe the man could have changed that much. He was acting too innocent *not* to be up to something!

He'd followed her instructions very well, leaving her alone, focusing his time and energies on Steve. The change in Steve had been amazing. She hadn't been aware of how subdued he'd been until he'd become more outgoing and self-confident since meeting Tony. Steve had definitely blossomed. Even her mother noticed the difference. He was much more relaxed around his grandmother now, gently teasing her, causing a flush of pleasure to appear from time to time on her pale cheeks. If her mother only knew who had caused the change! For some reason Steve had adopted a protective attitude toward his relationship with Tony where his grandmother was concerned, similar to the one Susan had had when they were growing up, but for different reasons. Steve knew his grandmother's opinion of sports in general and grown men making a living playing boys' games in particular. Susan had been amused to watch him diplomatically sidestep any subject that would necessitate Tony's name entering the conversation.

For example, Steve was willing to discuss scouting without ever alluding to the assistance he was receiving on several of his projects. No doubt she should say something to him, explaining that omitting certain facts was tantamount to lying. Somehow, she hadn't been able to bring it up, feeling anything she said would be too hypocritical since he'd watched her deal with her mother in the same way for years.

She turned off the water, stepped out of the shower and quickly dried off. Not bothering with makeup, she ran a comb through her hair and padded back into the bedroom to dress.

Steve was waiting for her. "Your breakfast is getting cold, Mom," he said with a touch of irritation.

"Sorry, Steve. Guess I'm moving at half speed this morning."

"Are you going to watch us build my racing car?"

"I hadn't given it much thought, why?"

"Just thought you'd want to see what we're doing," he said with elaborate unconcern.

"You bet I would. Wouldn't miss it for the world."

He grinned. "That's okay, Mom. I know you're really not into cars and things."

"It shows, huh?"

He nodded. "A little, but you do real well at the ballgames."

"I try," she muttered, and walked over to him. She gave him a big hug.

He struggled to get out of her grip. "You don't have to get mushy, Mom. C'mon. Let's eat."

Tony was waiting for them in the kitchen. Her

coffee was poured and waiting, as well as eggs, bacon and toast. She groaned. "I never eat that much for breakfast."

Tony stared at her with a stern look. "It shows. I'm going to put you on an athlete's training schedule, starting today."

Steve laughed. No one talked to his mom that way. He watched to see how she'd take it.

Susan sat down, surprised at the seriousness of Tony's command. Maybe she was pushing herself too hard and not eating correctly. She shrugged. It might be worth a try. Without a word she picked up her fork and started to eat.

Steve watched in amazement, then glanced at Tony, who winked at him. Obviously, this man had more influence over his mother than he'd given him credit for. It might be worth trying to pick up a few pointers.

Susan had long since wandered away from the intricate construction of Steve's race car when Tony finally called a halt. They sat back and admired it for a while, then Tony began to pick up his tools while Steve grabbed the broom to sweep up the sawdust.

Tony looked around, making sure everything had been put away, then walked over to Steve. "There's been something I've wanted to discuss with you, Steve," he began in a hesitant tone.

Steve replaced the broom on its hook. "Yes, Tony?"

"I'm not sure if this is the right time, but there's something I think you should know." He stood there watching the young boy, wondering how to approach the sensitive subject.

Steve walked over and stood by Tony. "What is it?"

"I want you to know that I'm in love with your mother."

Steve went from acute concern to laughter in the beat of a moment, his infectious chuckle causing a red stain to cover Tony's cheeks. "Why don't you tell me something I don't know?" he asked when he finally managed to stop laughing.

Doggedly, Tony continued. "I want to marry her."

Steve stuck his hands into his back pockets and rocked back and forth from his toes to his heels. "You got it really bad, huh?"

Tony nodded. "What would you think about my joining the family?"

Steve studied the serious expression on Tony's face. "You're really worried she won't marry you, aren't you?"

"That, and that you might be against the whole idea."

Steve grinned. "It isn't as if she doesn't know you, you know. You've known her longer than I have," he pointed out.

"That's true," Tony admitted carefully.

"She does seem to like you, I've noticed that," Steve added obligingly. "So when are you going to ask her?"

"That's what I thought I'd get your advice about. What do you suggest?"

"Well, how about tonight? Maybe after we eat I

can go watch television in the den and you can build a fire . . . you know, kinda set the scene . . . . then ask her."

"It sounds like you've given the matter some thought."

A suspicious flush appeared on Steve's cheeks. "Not exactly. That's the way they do it on all the mushy television shows." He crossed one foot over the other in an agitated movement. "That's usually when I go get something to eat," he confessed, making a face.

"Hmmm. That must be where I was, too. I didn't know that's how you went about it."

They started up the steps to the house. "Well, you can always try it and see if it works," Steve offered philosophically. "What have you got to lose?"

"What, indeed," Tony muttered to himself as they entered the house. Steve was right in one respect. There was no point in continuing to put it off. She must know how he felt about her; he'd never tried to hide his feelings where she was concerned. Instead, he'd tried to give her the space she seemed to need, to adjust to his presence in her life.

It was a very thoughtful Tony who began to make plans for the evening. He hadn't been this nervous before the last game in the World Series! But he knew in his heart Susan was worth more to him than any pennant. He only hoped he could find the words to convince *her* of that.

6

~oooooooooo~

The chilly wind swooping along the deserted beach finally forced Susan to give up her solitary walk. Even wearing one of Tony's heavy jackets with a hood hadn't prevented her hands and feet from turning into blocks of ice. But the walk had been worth the chilled fingers and toes.

She couldn't remember a time when she'd felt such peace. Her brief solitude had fed a hitherto unknown need buried deep inside. When had she last taken time for herself? Whenever she wasn't working, she'd felt a compulsive need to be with Steve. Her life seemed to be a series of commitments to fulfill other people's needs and expectations. But what of her needs?

By the time she reached the beach entrance to Tony's home, her knees felt like spaghetti and she was huffing and puffing like the wolf in the story of the three little pigs. Steve had always enjoyed her exuberant rendition of that scene, she recalled with a grin.

She glanced down the long stairway she'd just climbed. She was really out of condition. Tony was right. She needed to start taking better care of herself.

Her walk had helped her come to terms with her feelings where Steve and Tony were concerned. Why had she expected to be all things for Steve? No one person could fulfill such a role. She recognized that their lives would have been different if Michael had lived, but he hadn't. Instead, Tony had come.

The rapport between the two would be noticeable to the most casual observer. They were good for each other, and if she sometimes felt left out of their magic circle, she had only herself to blame.

She tugged open the sliding glass door that led into the living room. The house was quiet. *They're probably still in the garage working on that car.* She shook her head in amazement at their persistence. *Where do they get their patience?*

Pleasantly tired from her sojourn on the beach, Susan wandered into the bedroom she'd used the night before. The soft bed looked so inviting. It was only a few minutes past one—plenty of time for a short nap before she and Steve needed to leave. She sank down onto the luxurious softness of the bed and pulled the bulky comforter over her. A short nap, that's all she needed.

However, the unaccustomed exercise and fresh air

conspired with the warm cocoon of comforter and bed, and Susan fell into a deep, restful sleep.

The dark room confused her when she woke up hours later. She fumbled for the lamp by the bed. She couldn't believe the time—it was after six! She stumbled to the bathroom and splashed cool water on her face. *Why did I sleep so long?* she wondered. *Why didn't they wake me?*

She found them in the den, where Tony was showing Steve the strategies of backgammon. Their camaraderie touched her and for a moment she watched them—the unobserved observer.

Finally, she spoke. "Fine friends you guys are. You let me sleep away the entire afternoon!" She smiled to let them know she wasn't too concerned and strolled into the room, her hands in the back pockets of her jeans.

They both looked up at her in surprise, then Steve glanced at Tony uncertainly. "Were we supposed to wake you?" Tony inquired.

"Not really. I just prefer not to drive after dark, that's all, but it won't be the first time."

"But, Mom—" Steve's voice sounded anxious, but a glance from Tony caused him to be quiet.

Tony slowly came to his feet, stretching. Susan watched with fascination as his arms reached high over his head, his body sinuously easing the cramped muscles in his arms and shoulders. "I'm sorry," he said. "I assumed you knew you were invited to stay for the weekend. Dinner is almost ready—I would have called you before I let you sleep through our latest masterpiece."

Spend the weekend! The suggestion set off tiny alarms within her and she wondered if they could hear the jangling. Up until now their encounters had been short and casual, but a whole weekend together?

Frantically, Susan searched her mind for an excuse—any excuse. Then she remembered her bulky briefcase with a feeling similar to the one a battered boxer had when he finally heard the bell ending a round.

"I have a large stack of work to catch up on before Monday," she explained ruefully. "And since I was so busy all week preparing for the board meeting, I'm afraid I got behind with the rest of my work." She was pleased she'd thought of it. The work took on the qualities of an eleventh-hour reprieve—until Tony spoke.

"That's no problem. You can work in here all day tomorrow if you'd like." He gestured toward the walnut desk at one end of the room. "You won't be disturbed."

She stood there, staring at him helplessly. Now what? Steve's worried expression drew her attention. He really wanted to stay, that was obvious. What difference did it make where she worked? *Who are you kidding? Tony makes the difference. You aren't immune to him. Or have you forgotten?*

Tony waited for her answer, forcing himself to show only polite interest in her decision. *Don't push her!* he warned himself. He spotted the wariness in her eyes and felt a definite sinking sensation somewhere deep within. His chances of getting a positive response to his marriage proposal seemed to shrink in number.

Then she smiled—her beautiful, who-cares, let's-go-for-it expression that used to precede their most exhilarating adventures together. That was the person he remembered and was hoping to find. Her smile at that time seemed to be a good omen.

"Sure, why not? I take it that's all right with you, Steve?"

Steve caught Tony's eye and gave them both a big grin. "You bet, Mom." He jumped up and gave her a fast hug, then turned crimson. "Uh, think I'll get washed up to eat."

Never had a meal tasted so good. Susan couldn't remember when she'd eaten so much. Not since Mama Angelina was cooking for all of them, she was certain. The wine Tony had chosen was perfect, and by the time dinner was over, Susan felt very relaxed and mellow.

"Mom, is it all right if I watch television now?"

Susan stared at Steve in surprise. Why would he want to watch television when Tony was around? "What were you planning to see?" She and Hannah carefully monitored what shows Steve watched.

The cherubic expression on Steve's face might have warned her that his motives would not stand up to her scrutiny, but luckily for the plans he and Tony had made Susan was too relaxed to notice. "Jacques Cousteau has a special on."

She nodded. "If Tony doesn't mind, I don't."

Tony grinned. "No problem, Steve. You know where the television is—help yourself."

Susan had never seen Steve so eager to be gone. Perhaps the continual time spent in Tony's company was taking the edge off the hero worship, which was probably a good thing. A healthier, more realistic relationship could now develop.

"Why don't we go into the living room?" Tony suggested as he slid her chair away from the table. "We could sit in there and enjoy the fire and the quiet, if you'd like."

His hand rested lightly on her shoulder as they entered the room. The white foam of the waves was all that could be seen of the water, the muted roar of the incoming tide lending a pleasant rhythmic sound to the peaceful scene.

Tony flipped a switch and soft music filled the room. He motioned for her to sit down as he built up the fire until the flickering flames shot up once more in a mixture of bright colors. Susan became lost in the sight until Tony sat down beside her, placing two replenished wineglasses on the table in front of them.

"I rarely see you this relaxed," he murmured as he settled in next to her.

She smiled. "That's probably because I can't remember having been so relaxed in a long time." She glanced at him as she reached for her glass. "Thank you. It sounds trite to say I needed a break, but it's true." She sipped from her glass, then sighed contentedly.

He leaned back, his arm falling carelessly along the

back of the sofa behind her shoulders. "I've enjoyed having both of you with me, but then, I'm sure you already realize that."

Her head felt too heavy for her neck and she let it lean lazily against the warmth of his muscled arm and shoulder. "You're being very polite, and I appreciate it. But I'm very much aware that the amount of time you're spending with Steve definitely cuts into your romantic life."

"What makes you think so?"

"Because you're with him three or four times a week. I'm sure your female friends are wondering what you're up to."

"Is that your subtle way of asking me if I'm seeing someone?"

Susan sat up straighter, realizing that was exactly what she was doing and resenting the fact that he saw right through her. "I'm sorry. It's none of my business."

Tony slowly tightened his arm around her shoulder, turning her to him. "Would you like to make it your business?" he whispered. Then before she had a chance to answer him, Tony leaned down and kissed her, if the soft, tentative touch of his lips on hers could be considered a kiss. It was more of a question, the slight hesitation giving the impression of unsureness. But that was ridiculous—this man unsure of himself? Whether on the diamond or off, Tony Antonelli always seemed to know exactly what he was doing.

Being in Tony's arms felt so natural, for that moment Susan felt she was where she belonged.

That loosening of her reserve gave Tony all the encouragement he needed. With a soft moan he pulled her across his lap, nestling her in his arms and against his broad chest. His mouth captured hers, exploring, tasting, reacquainting them with the joys they had once shared.

Hesitantly, as though trying to find skills she had thought forgotten, Susan began to respond. Her hands slid tentatively across his chest, smoothing over the expanse of his soft sweater. Then they crept up around his neck and into his hair. She luxuriated in the feel of the curls that wrapped themselves tightly around her fingers.

Tony's kiss robbed her of all thought but him and his presence. As he reluctantly pulled away for air, Susan discovered that she, too, was out of breath. His hand trembled slightly as he stroked along her jaw. She rejoiced in knowing she affected him at least as much as he did her.

He kissed her once more, this time with a fiery passion that caught her unprepared. The possessiveness of the kiss caused such desire within her that she felt like a statue built of wax, melting from the heat. She responded with equal intensity and found herself being drawn down on the sofa, her body carefully aligned on top of his. His hands explored the contours of her spine, pausing and stroking across the gentle curve of her hips.

She could feel as well as hear the slight moan of pleasure he gave. Her sweater had long since pulled out of her slacks and she shivered when she felt his hand slide beneath her top, moving upward until it reached the clasp of her lacy bra.

The sudden feeling of her bare breasts as they rested against his chest seemed to bring Susan out of the daze she'd been in since dinner. What was she doing, necking on the couch while her son was in the next room? What was she thinking of? She stiffened as she acknowledged that was her problem. She hadn't been thinking at all—she'd been feeling—reacting—luxuriating in the closeness they shared, and had no business sharing. The past was over, and Tony Antonelli had no place in her future.

Tony felt her stiffen in his arms and he immediately paused. What was wrong? he wondered. She'd been with him every step of the way. What had changed her mind? He slowly eased his hand from underneath her sweater and began to caress her back in long, smooth strokes.

"What's wrong?" he finally asked.

Susan pushed herself up from her reclining position. Trying to hide the effect he'd had on her, Susan answered almost harshly. "Nothing's wrong. I'm a little old to be caught necking on the couch, that's all—particularly by my son."

Tony sat up, unconcerned that she could see how aroused he'd become. "I wouldn't do anything to embarrass you, Susan. I thought you knew that." He ran his hand through his already mussed curls. "In fact, I didn't intend any of this to happen."

She glanced around the dimly lit room, silently noting the fire, the soft music, and the beguiling view

117

of the ocean from the wide expanse of glass. "Didn't you?" She forced herself to look back at him, then wished she hadn't. His nearness was shattering to her already shaky composure. "I would say you have set up an excellent seduction scene."

Tony stood up and began to pace restlessly. "As a matter of fact, seduction was the last thing I had on my mind. My thoughts were much more old-fashioned."

She stared up at him, puzzled. When he didn't say any more, she prodded. "Old-fashioned?"

He paused, staring at her intently. "Susan, is there some reason why you're driving yourself by putting in those long hours?"

Whatever she had expected, his seemingly abrupt change of subject wasn't it. "What does my working long hours have to do with your necking with me on the couch?" she asked in a reasonable tone.

"Nothing, dammit. Or everything, maybe. Are you content with your life now? Is this how you intend to spend the rest of your days?" he demanded. "Working until your exhausted, squeezing in your extra time with Steve until you don't get enough rest? You don't eat right—you're entirely too thin. Is this what you want?"

His voice had grown steadily harsher as he talked, and Susan was bewildered. What had caused his change of mood? "Tony, why don't you sit down and tell me why you're upset."

"I'm not upset. I'm trying to find a way to ask you to marry me, but damn if I can come up with one.

You've made it clear you don't need me, or anyone, in your life. You have everything you want—a well-established career, a nice home, a fantastic son. Why should you want a man around?''

If he hadn't been so irate, she would have laughed. It was the strangest marriage proposal she'd ever heard of. He had very clearly listed all the reasons why she wouldn't accept him. Unfortunately, he was right, but then he'd always seemed to understand her better than she understood herself.

Susan stood up and walked over to him. "Tony, you know you're very special to me. We shared a childhood together that I'll never forget. You gave me Steve, whom I love better than my life." She touched him gently, resting her fingertips along his cheek. "I admire you tremendously for what you have done with your God-given talents. But our lifestyles are totally different. Can't you see that?''

Despite his strong intentions not to touch her, Tony's arms clamped around her waist, pulling her close to him. "Doesn't it matter that we still love each other?''

She shook her head slowly. "You don't love me, Tony. I doubt that you ever did, really. I was a symbol to you, one you worked hard to earn. But you don't know me as a person. If it weren't for Steve, you would never have bothered to look me up—I know that. He's your son and it's natural that you would want to claim him, but you don't need to marry me to do that. I know you love him, it's very obvious. But we aren't a package deal."

Never had he felt such frustration. Her calm and objective analysis of their relationship was masterly described—and dead wrong.

She was a symbol, all right, a symbol of everything he'd ever wanted in a mate. It never mattered to him who she was or what part of town she was from— she'd been his from the first moment he'd seen her. He'd waited years for her, working hard to be able to prove to the world that he deserved her, only to have her marry someone else. He loved her as he'd never loved anyone, and he felt certain she loved him as well. Why was she denying it?

She stood in his arms watching him, wondering what thoughts were causing the painful expression on his face.

"Oh, my love. You are much more than a symbol to me." With his hand he pressed her hard against his body while his mouth seductively made claim to hers. She was his. He just needed a little more time to convince her. *Please God, grant me that time, and the patience it will take to win her.*

Once again Susan was lost in the feelings that only Tony seemed to be able to evoke within her. What would it be like to be married to him? To wake up each morning with him? And then she remembered. She wouldn't be with him. He would be on the road for months at a time, and she had her law practice. His romantic exploits were legendary. Why would he be willing to give them up? He wouldn't have to, of course, and she wouldn't be able to live with that knowledge. Yes, she loved him, but she knew she could never marry him. The pain of knowing he wanted her for Steve would always stand between them.

But for the moment, holding him and loving him was enough. It would have to be.

Tony abruptly stepped back, releasing her. He reached over and picked up his glass of wine. *Well, you certainly blew that one, sport.* He drank from the glass, wondering what he could do or say that would get through the wall Susan had so carefully built around herself.

"I'm glad you came back to Santa Barbara, Tony," she said softly, sinking down once more on the sofa. She, too, reached for her glass, as though it were her composure to be clutched and regained. "You've been very good for Steve."

He glanced at her in surprise. Hesitantly, he stepped around the table in front of the sofa, and sat down facing her. "I'm glad to know you feel that way. Getting to know him has been the greatest thing that ever happened to me."

He reached over and took her hand, holding it loosely in his. "You know, there are nights when I lie awake, thinking back over all that happened, trying to picture our life together if I'd only known you needed me." He raised his hand, bringing her fingers to his lips and softly kissing them. "I'll never forget the day your mother told me you and Michael were engaged. I couldn't believe it. I kept thinking there had to be some mistake, and I had to get back and find out what was going on. When my roommate found me packing, he tried to talk me out of it, knowing I was throwing away my career if I walked out then. When reasoning didn't work, he tried to physically stop me and we got into one hell of a fight. The club fined us both. By then I was convinced you'd been stringing me along all that time, so we went out and got drunk, which cost another fine. It wasn't the greatest way to start my career. If it hadn't been for my roommate explaining what had happened, I'd probably been shipped home." His gaze rose from her hand and found her eyes. "Maybe then I would have still had you."

"Tony, it's so pointless to keep dwelling on what might have been. I've been doing some of the same thing, and it's a waste of time. If only I'd tried to contact you, or allowed Michael to call. The words *if only* are the two most useless words in our language, and the saddest. Please don't dwell on the past."

"Dammit, I'm trying to work on our future. I want you, Susan. I want to marry you. I want to be a husband to you and a father to Steve. Why won't you give me that chance?"

The compelling intensity in his eyes shook her to her very soul. All of her carefully marshaled reasons seemed to flit from her mind like wisps of smoke dissipating in a breeze.

"Don't you understand? We're too different. We want different things from life. I want peace and tranquility; you crave excitement and the adulation of the crowd. I couldn't handle that."

"You've got to be kidding me. Is that the way you see me, as some sort of overgrown Boy Scout, still playing childish games of baseball, not wanting to grow up?''

Her silence was an answer. He sat there and stared at her for a moment, then drained his glass. "You know what your problem is? You're afraid to live. You're afraid to enjoy life, to jump in with both feet and learn, and make mistakes, and grow. Instead, you've manufactured a nice little safe world for yourself, where there's no waves—and very little life. Well, that may be all right for you, but I'll be damned if I'll let you pull Steve into that stifling little world.'' He stood up, staring down at her with contempt. "You're right. I don't know you at all. The woman I've loved for most of my life probably doesn't even exist.'' He started for the door. "I'm going to take a walk. I'll see you tomorrow.''

Susan sat there staring at the fire long after he was gone. She had managed to convince him to her way of thinking. Why didn't she feel better about it? What was wrong with wanting a safe little world? Wasn't it better than pain and turmoil? Only with Tony had she been able to let go and experience the turbulent feelings of joy and ecstasy, and she'd paid dearly. She couldn't go through that another time. She didn't even want to try.

Tony jerked the cap from the pocket of his heavy jacket and jammed it onto his head. The wind had grown increasingly colder. It was no night for a stroll on the beach, but he had to get away.

What the hell was wrong with her? Couldn't she

see they belonged together? How could a woman so obviously intelligent treat her emotions as negligible? She loved him, he knew it. Otherwise, she wouldn't respond to him the way she did every time he took her in his arms. He had watched the pulse at the base of her throat as it fluttered restlessly during their conversation. She was not unmoved by him. He didn't care what she told him or herself.

Somehow he had to break through that shell. He just had to, not only for his sake, but for her sake and Steve's as well.

The question was, how?

7

~∞∞∞∞∞∞∞∞∞~

January brought increasingly frigid weather and Susan found it did not improve her disposition in the least. *What happened to sunny southern California?* she wondered waspishly as she drove home one Friday evening.

If she were honest, she'd admit that she hadn't been in a very good frame of mind since the weekend she and Steve had spent at Tony's home.

Tony was definitely becoming a problem. Not that he had ever brought up their discussion again. That she could have dealt with. Instead, he seemed to have moved into her home. He went home at night, but he was always there when she got home, had dinner with them or insisted on taking them out to eat. Steve and Hannah doted on him. Susan was counting the days until he had to return to Florida for spring training!

It was almost as though he had given up all thought of marriage, except for one new wrinkle in his behavior—he seemed to take great pleasure in touching her whenever he had the chance. He had an annoying habit of dropping a kiss on the end of her nose, or her cheek, and occasionally her mouth whenever he happened to pass her. And that seemed to be frequently. He didn't even seem to care who saw him do it. Both Hannah and Steve took it in stride. Susan wished she could learn to do the same.

However, that morning he'd finally overreached himself. It was bad enough that she felt she was continually tripping over him in her home, but when she found him in her bedroom, that was too much!

She had taken her shower and hadn't bothered to put on anything but her lacy underwear to enter the bedroom. When she walked out of the bathroom she found Tony stretched out on her bed.

"What are you doing in here?" she demanded, grabbing her robe.

"Waiting to talk to you."

"Well, you can wait in the other room. How dare you come in here!"

He grinned and Susan fought a strong urge to throw something at him. "You know, it doesn't seem quite fair that you and I should have shared something so intimate in order to create Steve and yet I've never seen you without clothes." He relaxed on the bed as though waiting for the show with keen anticipation.

"Tony! Get out of my bedroom. Now!"

"Okay, if that's the way you want it. I had hoped to talk with you in private, though."

She stared at him with suspicion. "About what?"

"The race car competition coming up next week."

A look of disbelief flashed across Susan's face. "You came in to my bedroom at seven in the morning in order to discuss the race car competition?"

"Um-hmmm." How could a person look so innocent while his eyes were so full of devilish lights?

"I'll meet you for coffee in the kitchen in fifteen minutes, Tony. Take it or leave it." She marched over to her closet and began to sort through hangers, trying to concentrate on what she planned to wear for the day.

In one lithe move Tony was off the bed and beside her. "Oh, I definitely intend to take it," he murmured. His arms slipped around her waist and he leaned down to her, his mouth finding hers in a soft caress.

Susan felt the heat of his body through her thin robe, the hard, muscular planes of his chest pressing against her. She recognized the warm liquid feeling that flowed through her body at his touch and for a moment allowed herself the luxury of enjoying his nearness.

His mouth explored hers as though reacquainting itself with each surface, his tongue stroking hers, his lips reshaping hers to fit perfectly with his.

"Mom, do you know where my—Oh, hi, Tony. I didn't know you were here. Did you spend the night?" The bright tone of speculation and interest was as effective as a bucket of ice water thrown over her. Susan jerked out of Tony's arms, appalled at the nonchalant attitude of her son. Why would he think she'd allow Tony to spend the night!

Before she could gather her wits about her, Tony was casually explaining. "No, I stopped in early enough to follow your mom to the garage. She's having her car worked on today and I'm giving her a ride to the office."

"Oh," Steve responded. "I didn't know anything was wrong with it."

"Neither did I," Susan offered in an annoyed tone.

The expression on Tony's face turned serious. "Susan, I've been telling you for the last several weeks you needed new brakes, and you've kept agreeing with me, but you haven't done anything about it. So I made an appointment for them to be repaired today."

How dare he be so high-handed! She was trying to find the words to wither his arrogance and over-bearing attitude when he dropped a hand on Steve's shoulder and guided him out of the bedroom door. "What were you looking for, sport?"

"My new jacket I got for Christmas. I've looked everywhere for it."

"When did you see it last?"

"I wore it home from school yesterday. Don't you remember?"

"That's right, so you did. Well, let's retrace your steps and see if you could have laid it down somewhere."

The two of them disappeared down the hallway, chatting, while Susan sank down on the bed, her knees trembling.

Something would have to be done. She couldn't let things go on this way. He was taking over their lives, slowly but surely working his way into their daily existence. It was going to have to stop.

She reiterated that statement through clenched teeth as she neared home that evening. The car drove like a dream. When the mechanic had brought her the keys about midafternoon, he explained that since he had the car in and Mr. Antonelli had told him to check it over, he'd gone ahead and tuned it, greased it, and changed the oil and filters. When she asked for the bill he explained it had already been taken care of—by Mr. Antonelli. "And he also gave me his autograph!" he'd added with a big smile.

She had a few very choice things she intended to tell Mr. Antonelli when she saw him again, and if he followed his customary schedule, he'd be waiting for her when she got home.

But he wasn't. Steve met her at the door with a long face. "Tony called and said he had to go out of town but he promised to be back by next Saturday for my race car competition."

Susan wasn't prepared for the sudden sinking feeling she experienced when she heard that bit of news. Damn the man! How dare he keep her feelings on a yo-yo string, jerked first one way, then another. She'd spent weeks refusing to grow accustomed to his presence only to discover she'd done just that.

She was glad he'd left! It was a good lesson for her. In little over a month he'd be leaving again, to be gone for months. This would be what she would have gone through had she been foolish enough to have agreed to marry him. Only it would have been much worse, for then she would have grown used to sleeping with him, waking up in the morning with him, making love with him. Now she was glad she'd kept her head and not given in to her emotions. Life was much easier if she didn't depend on anyone but herself.

By Monday she was more than ready to go back to work. Susan had grown tired of trying to cheer up Steve over the weekend. He'd finally spent most of Saturday with one of his friends, but Sunday he was back home wondering where Tony had gone, and why, and when exactly she thought he might be back, until Susan was convinced she would go out of her mind.

Hannah hadn't been much help, either. She'd pointed out how much Tony enjoyed her beef Wellington the last time she'd made it and that it was too bad he wasn't there on Sunday. The office was going to be a marvelous escape from reminders of Tony.

Unfortunately for Susan's peace of mind, it didn't work out that way.

At eleven-thirty Donna stuck her head around Susan's office door wearing a very peculiar expression on her face. "Susan, there's a delivery here for you."

Susan glanced up, surprised that Donna would interrupt her for such a common occurrence. Overnight deliveries in a law office were a customary procedure. "Can't you sign for it?" she asked, puzzled.

Donna's eyes grew larger. "Oh, sure, if you want me to." The obvious question in that last statement caused Susan to decide something strange was going on, so she got up and went out to Donna's office. A messenger stood there all right, but not from one of the regular services. He held a gigantic array of food. Upon closer inspection, Susan noted it was all health food, done up in various packages, sizes and shapes.

"Would you please sign here?" The man looked eager to be on his way. She couldn't blame him. He set the package down on Donna's desk and extended a receipt for her to sign. Susan recognized the name at the top of the receipt as a well-known health food restaurant.

After he left she and Donna eyed the food. "Here's a card," Donna volunteered. Just a corner peeked out from behind some freshly baked blueberry muffins, one of Susan's weaknesses.

Flipping the envelope open, Susan pulled out the card and read:

I don't want you falling off your eating just because I'm not there to keep an eye on you. You will receive a freshly prepared lunch each day until I get back. Make sure you eat it.

I love you,
Tony
P.S. And don't forget your vitamins!!

"I can't believe this," she muttered, sinking into the chair opposite Donna's desk.

"Who sent it?" her secretary asked.

"Who else? My health-nut friend. Tony."

"Tony Antonelli? Well, how very thoughtful of him. He obviously wants to see you put on some weight."

Susan studied the array of food before her with dismay. "Obviously."

"He must care a great deal about you to encourage you to eat right like that."

"You think so?"

Donna looked at her in disbelief. "Don't you?"

"At this point I don't know what I think, or if I think, or when I'm thinking. That man is driving me out of my mind."

Donna's face took on a dreamy expression as she rested her chin on the palm of her hand. "But what a way to go. . . ." she said softly.

By Friday Susan was convinced beyond a shadow of a doubt that one of them had lost their mind, but she wasn't sure whether it was Tony or her.

The food arrived on Tuesday as promised, but so did an ornately wrapped square box tied with a mammoth red bow. She studied the box warily. There was no logo or name that told her where it came from, but she had a suspicion as to who sent it.

She tried to work, ignoring the box as much as

possible, but when she realized she'd read the first page of the contract she was reviewing three times and still didn't know who the party of the first part was and what they were hoping to accomplish by the contract, it was time to face the inevitable. She wasn't going to be able to work until she knew what was in the box.

After making that decision it didn't take her long to remove the ribbon and paper, then open the top of the box, only to discover more tissue paper. When the last scrap was removed she found a baseball nestled inside a polished wood holder. It was ordinary enough, as baseballs go, except that every possible surface on it had been covered in a familiar handwriting. The words *I love you* were emblazoned all over it.

There was no card. The gift didn't need one.

On Wednesday Susan wasn't even surprised when Donna tapped on her door and with a big grin and announced, "You have another delivery." She tossed her pen on the desk and prepared herself for whatever awaited her.

Five men walked into her office, each carrying an outsize bouquet of flowers. They paused, looking at her inquiringly. She waved her arm at the various tables and desk top, where they began to place them around the room. She solemnly signed for the deliveries and waited until the men left before her sense of humor got the best of her.

She sat down in her chair and started laughing. The flowers caused the office to shrink in size, but that wasn't what Susan found so amusing. All of the ornate decorations were the type found at funerals. What was he up to now?

After searching three of the arrangements, Susan found the card.

It's better to be wed than dead. Don't bury those feelings. Admit you love me madly. Or at least a little. Please save me from my miserable single life. I need you desperately. (Would it help to remind you that I also love you to distraction?)
Your
Tony

Some comment and speculation had been expected when her hearty luncheons began to arrive each day, but the flowers brought everyone out of their offices to inspect and admire Susan's newly decorated room.

"Whoever he is, I admire his taste," Greg Bauerman admitted with a seductive smile. Greg was one of her partners who had spent considerable time attempting to console her after Michael's death. However, she had finally convinced him she didn't need his brand of consolation, and that perhaps his wife would better appreciate his thoughtfulness.

"Well, he certainly knows how to get your attention," admitted Jackie Lematta, one of the associates who worked in the corporate area with Susan.

"That he does, not to mention everyone else's in the office," Susan admitted.

When the furor died down and everyone went back to work, Susan recognized that for some reason she wasn't angry at Tony's flamboyant gesture. It was so in keeping with his personality, and his personality was one of the reasons she loved him so.

I really do love him, she finally admitted to herself with dismay. *I can no longer deny my feelings for him. But I am not going to marry him. It would be a disaster. My life is just the way I want it. Is it?* a little voice in her head asked. *Are you sure? Can you really walk away from what Tony is offering you?*

Just what is he offering me, anyway? Okay, he says he loves me, and maybe he does, during his off season when he's bored and at loose ends. But what about the rest of the year when he's involved with baseball and traveling and the adoration of his fans, especially the female kind? What about while I'm sitting here in Santa Barbara practicing law and raising Steve? He's stayed away from us for eleven years with no problem. There's no reason to suppose he'll feel any differently when he gets back into his other world.

A very subdued Susan went home that evening.

By midafternoon on Thursday Susan was convinced that Tony's dramatic offerings had come to an end. Lunch had arrived on schedule but nothing else had been delivered. Susan realized she'd been mentally holding her breath every time Donna brought something to her, waiting for his next move, and forced herself to relax.

Her concentration began to improve and the stack on her desk rapidly dwindled. She'd even managed to push Tony to the back of her mind, hoping to keep him there, when she heard Donna burst into unrestrained laughter. She'd breathed that metaphorical sigh of relief too quickly. Now what?

When she stepped into Donna's office, she flinched. She couldn't help it. The room appeared to be full to overflowing—with multicolored balloons! Not the sort of small balloons you see children holding at carnivals and circuses. No, these balloons were large, helium-filled balloons with writing on them. The writing was identical on each one: TONY LOVES SUSAN.

"Oh . . . my . . . God," Susan uttered as she sank down on the corner of Donna's desk.

"I went ahead and signed for them before he started bringing them in," Donna volunteered cheerfully. "It took him several trips. Shall I help you move them into your office?"

The move into her office wasn't anything like the struggle to get all of the balloons into her car that evening. The most embarrassing aspect was the drive home, with the balloons that wouldn't fit inside merrily bobbing their colorful heads outside, their strings securely tied together. She attracted more attention than newlyweds with tin cans trailing from their car.

She almost didn't go to work on Friday. Enough was enough. When she finally convinced herself that the coward's way was not *her* way, she was almost an hour late for work.

That's when Donna informed her one of her clients called and asked if she could come to his plant that morning. Could she! She'd be delighted. Whatever happened, she wouldn't be there to face it.

She spent a productive morning with her client, ended up having lunch with several members of management and returned to her office with a bounce in her step and a smile on her lips.

She paused at Donna's desk to pick up her messages. Her secretary appeared to be busy transcribing a tape and glanced up distractedly, then continued typing. Obviously, nothing untoward had happened in her absence. However, to be on the safe side she opened her door carefully and peeked in. The flowers were still there, and she had of course taken home the balloons yesterday. There seemed to be nothing new to be found today. She breathed a sigh of relief and walked in—and found Tony sitting on her couch.

"Tony! When did you get back?"

Her heart seemed to be doing somersaults in her chest and the air supply to her lungs suddenly became dangerously low.

He stood, and Susan absently registered how good he looked in his dark brown slacks and well-tailored shirt. "A little over an hour ago. Donna said she wasn't sure when you'd be back, but was kind enough to allow me to wait for you in here."

Susan didn't remember moving toward him or his coming to her. All she knew was she was in his arms again, and she couldn't remember when they had felt so good to her.

Her hands found their way through his hair, and her mouth sought his, eager to quench the thirst that a week away from him had caused within her.

His reception was more than he had hoped for,

but what he had longed and prayed for. Had he finally cut through her reserve? Was it time for him to push their relationship to its inevitable conclusion, the one that had been ordained years before when a lonely ten-year-old boy had looked into the clear blue eyes of a six-year-old girl, seeing the acceptance, feeling the rapport, yearning for the closeness of another human being?

His hands slid down her back and cupped her hips, pulling her closer against him. Her effect on him was almost instantaneous. He had spent the morning flight thinking of her, wondering if he dared go to her office, or if it would be better to wait and see her at her home. His final choice had been a selfish one—he didn't think he could wait the extra hours to see her.

He was glad he hadn't waited.

Their kiss was everything Susan had ever dreamed about—passionate, urgent and full of love. He was home. That was all that mattered—at the moment.

8

~~~~~~~~~~~~~~~~~~

"Look, Tony, they've got all our cars on display! Aren't they something?" Steve's excited voice carried over the noise of the milling people, causing several heads to turn.

Tony's arm was securely wrapped around Susan's waist, making it clear to everyone he was more than a casual friend.

She had dreaded today, even though she was careful not to let Steve know. It was his big day, the culmination of weeks and weeks of work. Today they would find out if his model race car was faster than all the rest. But for Susan it was a test of her ability to conceal her love for Tony.

Tony seemed to be as excited over the upcoming race as Steve. He visited with several of the fathers present, swapping stories of what they had done to make *their* race car different.

Tony glanced down at Susan and asked, "When are we supposed to eat, before or after the races?" His voice caused a ripple of awareness through her.

She glanced up and caught his warm gaze, and quickly looked away. "According to the posted schedule, they plan to have four heats before lunch, and the winners will compete after lunch—I packed something for us. Why, are you hungry?"

"A little. I skipped breakfast this morning."

Susan stopped walking and stared up at him in mock horror. "No! Not you, the man who insists breakfast is the most important meal of the day, the man who insists you are what you eat, the man—"

"All right, you've made your point. Let's just say that I overslept this morning and didn't have time to eat if I wanted to pick you two up by eight o'clock."

"You must have had a late night." She watched him with interest, curious to know what he had done after he left her house a little after ten.

A flush appeared on his cheeks. "It wasn't a late night, just a sleepless one." His gaze avoided hers.

"Oh, really? Now, why aren't you enjoying the restful sleep of the innocent?"

"You know damn good and well why not! After the good-night sendoff you gave me, promising so much, then backing off at the last possible moment, you actually wonder why I might have trouble sleeping? Even cold showers lose their effectiveness after the number of times I've been under one during the past few months." He glared at her. "You know I'm not used to living like this!"

"Like what?" she asked with wide-eyed innocence.

"Living without. And if you dare ask me 'Living without what?' with that sweet expression on your face, I may lose my reputation as a gentleman and show you right here and now." Since the last of that sentence had been muttered fiercely between clenched teeth, Susan decided she shouldn't continue to probe.

She certainly understood sleepless nights.

"C'mon, Tony. We're in the second heat. Let's go watch, okay?" Steve tugged on Tony's hand, oblivious to the stares of recognition around them. Tony might be a star in every one else's eyes, but at the moment he was Steve's moral support.

Susan watched as they hurried away. It never occurred to Steve to ask her to join them, but then, why should it? The project had been theirs—she'd had nothing to do with it. So why should she feel left out now? Glancing around the room, she noted the number of women looking out of place and ill at ease and recognized she was not alone.

At the moment she was in a male-dominated world and she might as well make the best of it.

"Did Hannah fry the chicken?" Tony asked, taking another bite from a crispy thigh.

"No, as a matter of fact, I did. Why?"

"You?" His eyes rounded with wonder. "Susan

Spencer McCormick can cook? I'm shocked. What ever would your mother say?"

She tossed a neatly cleaned chicken leg at him, where it bounced off his knee as they sat together at one end of the large room.

"Watch where you aim, lady," he scolded as he picked up the chicken leg and placed it with the scraps on his plate.

"It hit what I was aiming at," she explained. "Your knee."

"Right." He dusted off the crumbs from his thigh. "So when did you learn how to cook?"

She looked at him in surprise. "You're really serious, aren't you?"

"Sure I'm serious. Why would you ever bother? I know your mother never encouraged you to hang around the kitchen, and Hannah is certainly no slouch in that department."

Her mind traveled back over the years and the corners of her mouth rose softly. "I used to love to sit and watch Mama Angelina in the kitchen. She made cooking seem like a work of art. When she realized I was interested, she began to show me little things . . . how to chop vegetables, what to look for when buying fruit, the best cuts of meat to use for various dishes . . . and we went from there."

"You once mentioned that you used to take Steve over to see Mama. Did you ever tell her he was mine?"

"No, we never discussed it, but your mother always knew how I felt about you. When Michael and I suddenly married that summer I can remember seeing the pain in her eyes, but I was hurting, too, and couldn't talk to her about all that had happened. We were away at school when Steve was born, and by the time we returned you had bought her a home and she had moved. For the longest time I kept wanting to go see her, but I was afraid, until finally one day I couldn't stand it another moment. By that time Steve was about nine months old, crawling and full of energy. I bundled him up and went over there. I'll never forget it.

"I rang the doorbell and waited with Steve squirming in my arms. When she opened the door and saw us, her face lit up like a fireworks display. I threw my free arm around her neck and hugged her, then said, 'I brought Steve over to meet you, Mama Angelina. He needs you as much as I always have.' I pulled his little cap off and his curls fell across his forehead. He looked at her with those big black eyes of his and she gasped. She knew, Tony . . . oh, she knew. Her hands were shaking and she took him out of my arms and held him to her, crooning and crying, until he pulled away from her. All she said was 'Oh, Susan,' and she said that several times, shaking her head, tears pouring down her cheeks.

"But we never discussed it. She just asked me when I left that day when I was coming back and I told her I would come as often as she wanted me. Tears filled her eyes and she shook her head impatiently and said, 'You come anytime you can. You know I love you like my own. And now I also have Stephen to love as well.'"

Susan was quiet for several minutes, the low

murmur of the many voices in the room only a background for her memories. "When we weren't in school I spent a part of each day with her, so that she could get to know Steve, and he could learn to know her as well. She spent much of our time together teaching me how to prepare meals, even though we had Hannah. But I found it very soothing to work in the kitchen, and it made me feel closer to her, somehow."

When she looked at Tony she could see the pain etched on his face. "She never told me," he said in a low voice. "She never once mentioned you, or Steve, or what had happened." He ran his hand through his hair. "She must have blamed me."

"Why do you say that? She could just as well have blamed me."

He turned his gaze slowly until he was facing her. "Otherwise, she would have told me about his existence."

"I don't believe that was her motive. I think she figured if you didn't know about him it was because I hadn't told you, and she was going to stay out of it. I don't think your mother ever placed blame on people. I think she just accepted us, and loved us, don't you?"

"God, I hope so. I would hate to think she was hurt over what she must have seen as my irresponsibility. I had no business leaving you alone to face the situation by yourself. Believe me, I've paid for that poor judgment. I'm just wondering how much longer you're going to make me pay."

"What do you mean, I make you pay? I'm not

blaming you for what happened. How many times do I have to say that?"

"Then if you aren't blaming me, why won't you marry me?"

"Tony! This is supposed to be a picnic lunch at a race car exhibition. Why are you bringing this up here?"

He shook his head, glancing around at the other people as though they had just materialized. "You're right. This isn't the time or the place, but the question is valid. I need an answer from you . . . and soon."

They cleared up their picnic remains, found Steve with one of his friends, and stayed the afternoon watching the rest of the races. Steve's car was eliminated on the second heat, but he'd had the thrill of winning the first one and seemed to be satisfied.

It was on the way home that Tony announced he had managed to get three tickets to see the Lakers play the following night. Steve was ecstatic. "That's great, Tony. How did you do it? I heard they've been sold out for weeks."

"Oh, I happen to know a fellow who owed me a favor. Anyway, we'll need to leave tomorrow afternoon to get there in time to find a place to park and eat before the game."

"Oh, Tony, I don't think I'd better go," Susan tried to say.

"Why not?" His tone was almost belligerent. "You don't care for basketball, either?"

"What do you mean, either?"

"I'm aware you don't approve of baseball, but I didn't realize your aversion covered all sports."

"That isn't true. I do like baseball."

"Funny, that's not the impression I get."

"Tony, did you guys have a fight or something? You sound awfully grouchy," Steve offered from the backseat.

"Sorry," Tony muttered, then in a voice too low for Steve to hear, he added, "That's what frustration does to you, among other things!"

Susan stared at him in the light from the passing cars. Steve was right. He sounded grouchy . . . he even looked grouchy. She reached over and patted his thigh, causing him to flinch, then glare at her. In her meekest voice Susan offered, "I'm sorry. I'd be happy to go to the game with you and Steve tomorrow."

Sunday turned out to be a beautiful day. The air seemed warmer to Susan, giving off hints of spring, even though it was barely February.

Steve was excited about seeing the Lakers play for the first time. She recognized another part of his education she had neglected, but it hadn't even occurred to her to try to take him to more sports events.

"How about lunch, sport? Think you can find room after the breakfast you managed to put away?" Tony ruffled Steve's curls and got a big grin for his efforts.

"Probably," Steve admitted.

They found a Mexican restaurant and Susan noticed that, like Steve, she wasn't having any trouble making a dent into the luncheon special she'd been served. Since Tony's arrival into their lives she had definitely put on weight. But she had to admit that she not only looked better, she felt much better. Notwithstanding the frustration of kissing him good night each evening and going to bed alone, she admitted to herself she was even sleeping better.

However, her dreams had definite erotic overtones to them.

"We'd better hurry, Tony," Steve insisted, "or we're going to miss the beginning of the game."

The coliseum was packed by the time they found their way to their seats, and Susan was glad to sit down. Tony had kept a tight hold on her hand as they wended their way through the crowd, and as soon as they sat down, his arm was around her shoulders.

It was not surprising to Susan that Tony had been recognized and stopped numerous times, accepting congratulations and listening to sports fans air their opinions on various rulings and calls. What surprised Susan was the way she seemed to be accepted as part of Tony's life. Tony made sure that both she and Steve were not jostled away from him in the crowd, and she felt very protected.

By the time they got back to the car after the game was over, Susan couldn't wait to kick off her shoes and relax. They had a long drive home, but seeing Steve's excitement and enjoyment had been worth it. He didn't ask for much from anyone, and he had an innate ability to appreciate everything that was offered him.

She gave Steve a big hug before stepping back

and letting him crawl into the minuscule backseat of Tony's sports car.

"What was *that* for?" Steve asked as he got in.

"Oh, I just felt like it. Isn't it all right for a mother to hug her son once in a while?" she answered, sitting down and closing the car door.

There was a thoughtful silence from the back of the car. Finally, a grudging voice admitted, "I suppose. Just don't make a habit of it."

She knew if she glanced at Tony, who was watching traffic, ready to pull out if he got a chance, she would burst into laughter. *That's part of the fun of sharing your child's antics with another person. No one, with the exception of the other parent, could possibly appreciate some of the comments and actions of your offspring. I'm glad Tony is here tonight.*

Steve was sound asleep by the time they hit the Ventura Freeway on the way home. Susan laid her head against the neck rest and found herself dozing.

"Susan?" Tony's low voice rumbled into the silence of the car. She rolled her head lazily toward him.

"Hmmm?"

"I didn't know how to tell Steve, so I haven't. But I have to leave for Florida this week. I should have left this weekend, but I couldn't leave Steve before his race car was tested."

She'd known he was leaving. She'd known it was this month. So why did she have such an empty feeling in the pit of her stomach?

"Aren't you going to say anything?"

She stared at his profile, silhouetted by the lights on the dash. His jaw looked clenched, his face almost grim. "What do you want me to say?" she asked in a soft voice, aware of the boy asleep behind them.

"You could say *something,* like 'I'm going to miss you, Tony—'"

"I *am* going to miss you, but you already know that."

"Do I? How would I know? You continue to treat me as some casual neighbor, one of Steve's little friends come to play."

"Hardly *little,* Tony," she murmured with a sleepy smile.

"How about saying, 'I love you, and I've changed my mind about marrying you.'"

The silence after that remark became deafening as Susan refused to say what was in her heart, determined to stick to the decision she'd made.

After a while Tony sighed, a defeated sound that pierced her. "All right, Susan, we'll play this game by your rules. But I think you're making a big mistake."

"Perhaps I am, but it *is* my decision."

"That may be true." He paused. "Obviously, it's true, but have you faced how your decision affects both me and Steve? I love him. I want to be with him. I want to be able to have him with me from time to time, show him the sights of some of the cities I've visited. I want you there with me, too. Doesn't that count for something?"

"Tony, please don't wake him up. Look. I understand how you must be feeling." She ignored his snort of disbelief. "But you have to look at it from

149

my point of view. We have a quiet, stable existence here. It has been good for both of us to feel secure in who we are and what we are. Here we are our own persons. With you or around you we become part of Tony Antonelli's entourage."

"Is that what all of this is about? You're afraid you're going to lose your identity if you're married to me? C'mon, Susan, you're more secure than that!"

"What I'm saying is that life on the road is too unstable for either me or Steve, and staying in Santa Barbara while you're gone for months at a time won't work either."

"Why do you have to look at it as an either-or situation. Why can't we have the best of both worlds? You don't need to spend the entire season moving around with me, but you could fly and meet me whenever Steve had time off." He reached over and placed his hand over both of hers, lying clenched in her lap. "Please don't push me out of your life again, love. I don't think I could stand it."

They were both quiet the rest of the way home, each deeply buried in thought.

Steve managed to wake up enough to get out of the car and stumble up the walkway into the house. With Susan's help he stripped off his clothes and fell into bed. *He probably won't even remember coming home,* she thought with a soft smile as she tucked the covers around him and switched off the bedside lamp.

Tony was waiting for her in the living room, sipping on a drink as he sprawled at the end of one of the sofas. He waved at another glass of wine sitting on the table next to him. "Come join me for one last drink together, then I've got to go. I've still got packing to do and my flight leaves at six in the morning."

Her legs refused to support her weight and she plopped down beside him. "You're leaving *tomorrow?* You said you had to leave sometime this week!" Tony didn't miss the tone of accusation and dismay, but hid his feeling of satisfaction from her.

"Tomorrow is sometime this week, Susan. Most everyone else is down there today. I was given a twenty-four-hour extension. I can't abuse it."

He set his glass on the table and turned to her. "I'm a glutton for punishment, you know. I would very much like something to take with me over the next lonely months, a memory of you in my arms." He grinned, that heartstopping expression that caused her to melt. "Hell, I've grown so accustomed to those damn cold showers, I'd probably miss them if I didn't need them."

Why resist him when she didn't want to in the first place? In the second place, there were some memories she needed to store up as well.

His kiss made it clear he was hungry for her. His mouth was hot and passionate, turning her bones to liquid and her mind to putty. She tugged at his shirt until it came out of the snug waistband of his pants, then ran her hands along his muscled back, stroking over his shoulder blades and down his spine.

She heard his moan of appreciation and her heartbeat quickened. When his lips finally left hers she could see the hot desire in his eyes and at that moment she knew she would not deny Tony anything. She loved him. She'd always loved him. And he was leaving her tomorrow.

She still had tonight.

Susan made no move to stop him when he brushed her blouse from her shoulders, slipped off the straps of her teddy and slid his hands down her waist, leaving her bare.

"Dear God, Susan, you're beautiful."

For the first time since she could remember, she felt beautiful. She saw the love and desire he felt for her and she was complete, a woman wanted and needed. She unbuttoned his shirt and pushed it away, wanting to feel that wide, muscled expanse after all these months of denial. She explored the soft mat of dark hair covering his chest, her fingers lightly outlining his heavy shoulder muscles. She kissed him at the base of his throat, her tongue licking him lightly, and she felt his convulsive jerk at her touch.

This was what she wanted, what she'd waited for, and she no longer cared about anything, not even that Steve was in the next room. All she knew at the moment was that Tony was leaving, and that after tonight she would be alone.

He traced a line of kisses from her mouth, down the side of her neck, onto her collarbone, then paused. His hands cupped her breasts, their tautness reassuring him she wanted him as much as he wanted her. Once again his mouth moved lower, tentatively kissing her, his tongue touching her on her delicate curves until she thought she would cry out with wanting him.

She sighed with relief when his mouth found the crest of her breast, and while his tongue gently explored her, his hands caressed her body in long, inflammatory strokes. He wrapped his arms around her and they sank down onto the sofa. This was what she'd been missing all these years—the feel of Tony's body pressed urgently against her, the scent of him surrounding her, the warm taste of him against her lips.

Their kisses became deeper and more soul-stirring. She felt as though she'd been created to love this man and all she wanted at the moment was to please him.

His hands touched her with unbelievable delicacy, gently exploring her innermost secrets. The feel of his aroused body shot flames of joy and unleashed desire through her. She loved him. Oh! How she loved him. And for tonight she could pretend they belonged together. Their remaining clothes disappeared as they both strove to get closer, ever closer, to each other.

Tony realized there would be no turning back. She was his for the taking. No longer an innocent child, she knew what she was doing. She wanted him every bit as much as he wanted her. Whether or not she admitted it to him, he knew she loved him, had known for weeks. Now she was giving herself openly and honestly. Again. *My God! It's happening all over again, just like eleven years ago.* He shook his head like a boxer who'd just received a blow to the head. *I can't go through that again!*

Susan had long since lost control of her thoughts.

She only had the ability to feel, to react, to rejoice in their closeness. This was Tony, and she wanted him, desperately.

She felt his body stiffen, and she clutched him to her, trying to convey the message that it was all right. She wanted him to make love to her. She needed his love.

And then he was pulling away from her. With jerky movements accompanied by harsh breathing Tony reached down and grabbed his pants, stepped into them and stood up, pulling them up to his waist and fastening them.

"Tony?" Susan looked up at him, bewildered. He glanced at her quickly, then away. He couldn't afford to look at her now or he couldn't do what he had to do. He had to make it clear to both of them that things were no longer the same. They had both changed. He couldn't take her, then leave her as he had before. "What's wrong?" she whispered.

He searched for an explanation. He couldn't fight both of them on this. He needed her help. "I'm good enough to go to bed with, just not good enough to marry, is that it?" His voice sounded harsh, because his breathing was still so labored.

His comment had the desired effect. She stared at him as though he had slapped her. She sat up and looked around dazedly. Her clothes lay scattered around her. She found her slacks and slipped them on again. Her blouse was a wrinkled wad on the couch, but she grabbed it up anyway and with shaking fingers managed to button it.

Staring at the man standing only a few feet away

from her but miles away in understanding, Susan said the only thing that came to mind. "I love you, Tony."

The contempt on his face made her cringe. "You have a strange way of showing it. You've deprived me of my son, but you're willing to take the chance of another pregnancy." He ran a hand through his hair. "Well, sorry, sweetheart, I haven't stooped to stud service yet. Okay, so you don't want to marry me. I guess I'll accept that. You don't give me any choice. But I'll be damned if I'll have an affair with you." He grabbed his jacket off the back of the chair and strode toward the door. "Tell Steve I'm sorry I didn't tell him good-bye, but I'll be calling him." He stopped and stared at her for a moment, memorizing her. She still stood by the couch, watching him helplessly. Her hair tumbled around her shoulders and down her back, her fuller figure curved enticingly, and he realized once again how much he was giving up by walking out the door. But he had his own self-respect to deal with. He loved her. He wanted to marry her, and he wasn't going to settle for anything less.

"Tony—" She held up a hand as though to beg him to stay, and he knew he couldn't wait any longer or even his self-respect would be thrown out the window.

"Good-bye, Susan. Hope you enjoy your safe little world. Maybe it will keep you warm nights."

She watched him open the door, step through, then gently close it. A slamming door would have been a much better punctuation to his statement.

Somehow the gently closing door seemed so quietly final.

Tony was gone, just as she knew he would be. She had held out, knowing she was right in her decision. Her face felt wet and Susan realized that tears were streaming down her cheeks. How long had she been crying?

Tony was gone. Tony was gone. Tony was gone. She undressed to the rhythmic refrain, and for the next several weeks her life continued to the beat of those words.

Tony was gone.

9

Susan stared out the window of her office at the sunshine. It was the second week in April and Tony had been gone two months. He'd left an empty hole in her life and her heart still throbbed with pain. She missed him terribly, and it didn't seem to be getting better.

He'd kept his word and stayed in touch with Steve. He called often, usually between the time Steve got home from school and Susan came home from work. It was obvious that he didn't want to speak with her. He was keeping the spirit as well as the letter of their agreement made last fall—he would stay close to Steve and out of her life.

That was the way she wanted it, wasn't it, the way she had insisted it must be? Only now she wasn't so sure and she was very much afraid it was too late to change it.

She wandered out to her secretary's desk. "Have I had any calls?"

Donna looked up in surprise. "No. Was I supposed to be holding them for you?"

"No, it just seemed so quiet around here, I thought I'd check."

Donna waved a hand at the window. "We're probably the only ones still inside on such a beautiful day. Everyone else is out somewhere enjoying the sunshine."

"I was thinking the same thing. Steve has a game after school tomorrow and I was hoping the nice weather would hold."

Donna watched her for a moment, puzzled. "Is there anything wrong?"

"No, of course not. Why do you ask?"

"Oh, I don't know. It's just that I've worked for you for over three years and this is the first time we've ever sat around and discussed the weather." She grinned. "So what did you think about Tony's interview on television last night?"

Susan refused to lie and say she hadn't seen it when in fact she, Steve and Hannah were glued to the set for a full hour before his appearance was scheduled to make sure they didn't miss it. "I thought it went quite well."

"Oh, so did I. Particularly when he refused to discuss the reason he's no longer vying for the title of Don Juan of the Diamond this year."

Susan could feel the heat in her cheeks. "Well, I

guess I'd better get back to work," she said, trying to ignore Donna's knowing smile. She returned to her office only to end up standing in front of the window, staring out.

She had thought Tony looked tired and she wondered if he was getting enough rest. It had been so good to see him and she'd found herself studying him intently, looking for any changes, hoping he was all right.

She had to get him off her mind or she was going to go crazy. Just then the phone interrupted her thoughts and she eagerly went back to her desk to answer it.

"Susan McCormick."

"Oh, Susan!" Hannah's voice sounded distracted.

"What's wrong, Hannah?"

"Steve was about a block from home on his bike just now when some idiot made a corner too wide and went into the other lane—"

"Steve was hit by a car?" She sank slowly into her chair.

"Yes. A neighbor came and got me and by the time I got there the ambulance was already on the scene. They told me to have you meet them at the hospital."

"How bad is he?"

"They wouldn't say. All I know is that he was unconscious."

Susan was already scrambling for her purse in the bottom drawer of her desk when she said, "I'll see you at the hospital."

As she ran through Donna's office, she said, "Call

my dad and have him meet me at the hospital. Steve's been hurt.''

Donna was already dialing before Susan had finished speaking.

Susan could scarcely recall later the drive to the hospital. She remembered being thankful it was only a few blocks from her office, and that traffic was so light. She remembered the orderly confusion of the hospital with the heavy traffic flow in the hallways near the emergency area and the quiet efficiency of the staff.

What she best recalled was Dr. Masters explaining what he'd found after examining Steve and allowing Susan to see him. "He regained consciousness while we were cleaning him up,'' he reassured her, "and he recognized me.'' He glanced down at the sleeping child. "His cuts and bruises look worse than they are. There should be no problem healing. What I'm concerned about is possible internal injury. I'm recommending that you give us permission to do some exploratory surgery. I don't like some of the vital signs. They point to some problems in the abdominal area.''

She stared at him, wondering what he expected from her. If he thought surgery was necessary, how could she argue with him?

"Whatever you say, Doctor. You know what's best.''

"I'll let you know as soon as I find out anything.'' He patted her shoulder reassuringly, then led her out into the hallway. Motioning to another door, he said,

"Why don't you wait in there for now?" Then he disappeared behind the doors marked SURGERY. She found Hannah in the waiting room, calmly crocheting an afghan and for a flash Susan wished she had the patience for handwork of some sort. She sank into a chair and they began their vigil.

Hours later she was still waiting for news. Her mother and dad had joined them and she sat hunched over, her father's hand clenched between hers.

"Why don't we go get some coffee, Susan? I think it would help you to move about."

"I can't, Daddy. I don't want to miss Dr. Masters. Why is it taking so long? What are they doing?"

"Baby, exploratory surgery is just what it sounds like. They aren't sure what they're looking for, and it takes time. You don't want them to hurry and overlook something, do you?"

"No. I just want him to be all right."

"We all want that, love. Just be patient a little while longer." He stood up. "I'll go get some coffee for all of us."

Susan's mother sat across the room from them, alone in her grief. She had always insisted she could handle things without help and now was unable to either give or take comforting. But she was suffering.

Susan heard the slight whooshing sound as the door closed behind her father, and she felt as though she were held in some sort of suspended animation while she waited for his return.

When she heard the door again, she glanced up, but it wasn't her father.

"Tony!" Susan hadn't cried when she heard the news about Steve, nor when she'd gone through the routine of admitting him, waiting in the emergency area, nor when she learned he needed surgery. But seeing Tony seemed to knock all her composure from her. By the time she got to her feet he was there and she grabbed him, wrapping her arms tightly around his waist, her head burying itself in his chest. "Oh, Tony," she managed to say, "I'm so scared."

"I know, love, I know. How is he?"

"We don't know anything. He's been in surgery forever, it seems."

"Surgery? Why?"

"Internal injuries." She shuddered. "He also had several cuts and bruises around his face and arms, but the doctor said they aren't serious. There's a possible concussion." She clutched him closer. "Oh, Tony, he looked so terrible . . . and so small!"

"What are *you* doing here?" Marsha Spencer's voice sounded too loud in the otherwise quiet room. Of course she recognized him. He hadn't changed very much from the boisterous, troublesome child she had known. But this was the last place she ever expected to find him.

Before Tony had a chance to respond, Susan's dad walked through the door with the coffee. "I called him. He needed to be here, Marsha, and you might as well understand that now. Steve belongs to Tony as much as he does to Susan and he has as much right to be here as either of us does."

Stephen Spencer met the steady gaze of the man who held his daughter, then gave a slight nod of approval at his presence. He sat down by his wife. "The important thing at the moment, Marsha, is that a young life hangs in the balance in the other room. All of us love him, and he needs all the help and prayers he can get."

Marsha Spencer sat as still as a marble statue, her color resembling one also. She stared at the couple still standing in the middle of the room holding each other, as though she'd never seen either of them before in her life. "But Michael and Susan—"

"It was never Michael and Susan, my dear, except in your own mind. It was always Tony and Susan." Stephen Spencer's clear blue eyes gazed at his wife calmly. He took her cold hand between his two warm ones. "It will all come out all right, Marsha, don't worry. We don't need to make their decisions for them."

Marsha stared at the kind, loving face of her husband and sighed. Slowly she dropped her head on his shoulder and visibly relaxed.

Susan pulled back slightly from Tony. "Thank you for coming. I need you so much."

"I got here as soon as I could. I wanted to come. When the emergency call came in I left right away and chartered a jet to get here. I only wish I'd had enough sense to do something like that eleven years ago!"

"Don't, Tony. It no longer matters. What's important is that we're together now." Her voice caught on a sob, and she prayed she wasn't too late with her decision for the three of them.

It was almost as though Tony knew what she was thinking. "He's going to be all right, love. He's in good hands in there, and he's in God's hands as well. We'll make it together as a family yet."

Another hour went by before the door quietly opened once more. Dr. Masters stood before them in his surgical greens, his mask lying loose around his neck, a wide smile on his face. "He's going to be fine."

The response to his statement was audible and varied. All five people waiting had stood as soon as they saw him, and the "Thank Gods" and cries of joy prevented anyone from saying anything else for a few moments.

"What did you find, Doctor?" Tony finally asked.

"We found a few tears in his intestines, which is what took so long. It took time to find them, then suture them, and make sure we'd gotten everything. He's going to have to be in the hospital for a spell, waiting for them to heal, but he'll have an interesting scar to impress his friends. Hopefully, he'll feel it's an even trade."

"When can we see him?" was Susan's first coherent question.

He glanced at the clock on the wall. It was after ten. "He won't be out of surgery for a little while yet. They're just finishing up. He'll probably be in the recovery room until morning." He glanced at the people gathered around him. "Why don't you go home and get some rest?"

"But doctor—" Susan's mother began, only to be quieted by her husband. He dropped his arm around her shoulders.

"He's right, my dear. We all need our rest. Let's go home now. It's been a rather hard day for you."

They walked out the door together.

"C'mon, Susan," Tony said, "I'll take you and Hannah home. You've had a pretty hard day yourself."

Hannah looked up from her crocheting. "That's all right, Tony. You take Susan on home. I've got my car whenever I decide to leave, but I think I'll stick around a while." She stared up at the doctor with a determined smile.

Dr. Masters laughed. "You were always a stubborn woman, Hannah."

"You should know," she retorted. "You're the one who recommended me to take care of Steve when he first arrived."

"I know, and I should have known better than to expect anything different now. You're worse than a mother hen with one chick."

"No I'm not, but I know I won't sleep anyway, so I might as well stay here for a while. Would it be possible for me to sit in his room?"

The doctor shrugged. "I certainly won't try to stop you. I'll leave word at the nurses' station that you're his private-duty nurse."

She smiled. "Thank you."

He shook his head and turned to Susan and Tony. "As though I had much of a choice."

"Are you sure I shouldn't stay, too?" Susan asked.

"Not you, too. You know there isn't a thing you can do for him tonight. You're going to need all the rest you can get for when he wakes up tomorrow. Trying to keep that young man flat on his back is going to take some doing."

"He's right, you know," Tony murmured. "Let me take you home."

The doctor followed them into the hallway. Tony turned and stuck out his hand. "Thank you for everything, Doctor."

Dr. Masters took his hand in a firm grip. "You've got a fine young man there, Tony. I know you must be very proud of him."

Tony's arm tightened around Susan's shoulders. "We are."

They watched as the doctor turned away. Then Tony and Susan began the long walk down the quiet hallway that led them to the world they'd known before the accident.

Susan stood before her bathroom mirror, slowly pulling the pins from her hair. Her head ached so, and it felt good to ease the tight pins out of the loop of hair at the nape of her neck.

"Here, drink this." Tony stood in the doorway of her bathroom, holding a brandy snifter out to her.

"I don't want anything to drink, Tony. I'm fine."

"I know. But drink it anyway. Why don't you hop in the shower while I look for something to eat? I'm sure Hannah has plenty in there." He turned around and headed out of the room. She heard her bedroom door close softly behind him.

By the time she walked into the kitchen Tony had reheated some homemade soup and had prepared a stack of sandwiches. "I realized I hadn't eaten for the last several meals and time zones, so I made enough for both of us." He looked up from stirring the soup and stopped talking. She looked like the young girl he had grown up with—her hair cascaded over her shoulders, her face was flushed from the hot steam of the shower and her bare toes peeked out from under her blue robe. "Where are your slippers?"

She looked around the room vaguely. "I don't know. I couldn't find them."

"Then put on some socks or something. There's no sense in your getting sick at a time like this, is there?"

She nodded obediently, and went in search of footwear. He shook his head. God, how he loved her, and if her reception of his presence was any indication, he hoped that eventually she was going to admit that she needed him as much as he loved and needed her. But not tonight. It was enough that she accepted his presence. He'd learned patience the hard way. He didn't intend to push for any declarations now.

"You aren't planning to drive out to your place tonight, are you?" she asked after she'd eaten. He was glad to see she still had a decent appetite. Not all of his winter's labors had been ignored.

"Sure, it's not all that far."

"But it's senseless to drive all that way when we need to be at the hospital early tomorrow." His heart bounced at the use of the word *we,* as though their going together were a foregone conclusion. "With both Hannah and Steve at the hospital, there are two extra beds."

"We'll see."

She looked at him imploringly. "Please stay, Tony. I don't want to be alone tonight, okay?"

His heart took two giant leaps, then settled sedately back in its proper place once more. When she looked at him like that, he'd promise her anything! "All right, if you insist."

She yawned, then gave him a sleepy smile. "I insist. I really *didn't* need that glass of brandy, Tony. I'm so relaxed, I'm about to fall out of this chair."

He stood up suddenly and scooped her up in his arms. "We can take care of that problem right now. It's past your bedtime, woman." Her arms obligingly wrapped around his neck and he strode down the hallway toward her room. Placing her carefully on the bed, then pulling the covers back, he said, "I suppose you can get yourself ready from there," and began to back toward the door.

She looked up at him with sleepy dismay. "You aren't even going to kiss me good night?"

He had only so much in the way of will power, and it was already being tested to the limits. "Not tonight, love. I'll see you in the morning." He turned away.

"Tony?"

He knew better than to turn back. Her soft voice had jolted through him like a series of electrical charges. He had never heard that particular entreaty in her tone before.

He stopped, turned slowly and leaned on the doorjamb for support. The soft lamp by the bed cast a halo around her. She stood by the turned-down bed, her robe a puddle of blue satin around her feet. The light behind her lovingly outlined her soft curves through the sheer fabric of her nightgown.

"What is it, love?" he finally managed to get out.

"Please stay with me tonight."

His tone was harsh with his effort at self-control. "I told you I would."

"I mean here." She gestured toward the bed. "With me." Before he could interrupt she said, "I need to know you're here, Tony. All I want you to do is hold me."

All she wanted! Her eyes melted any resistance he had left. He shrugged and started toward her, absently unbuttoning his shirt.

"You realize what you're saying, don't you?"

She nodded, her face solemn. "Yes. I love you, Tony. I always have . . . I always will. It's like a permanent condition within my body that nothing can seem to destroy." She could hardly speak for the lump in her throat, but she tried for lightness. "I was hoping your marriage proposal was still open for consideration. . . ."

The look on his face caused her voice to fail. It was as though a light had flashed on deep within him. He glowed. There was no other word for it.

Then he was beside her. His hand trembled slightly as he placed it along her cheek. "Oh, Susan,

169

love, I had almost given up hope of ever hearing you say that to me." His arms came around her in a tight clasp and the kiss he gave her expressed all the love—and the pain—he'd felt for so long. It was a possessive kiss, a kiss filled with commitment, and caring, and promises he vowed to keep.

He slid the straps of her nightgown from her shoulders and the soft material slithered down to rest lightly around her hips. His hands slipped to her firm breasts, caressing them with tenderness.

Susan could no longer resist touching him and she reached for his shirt, sliding it off his shoulders. Before he could slip his arms out of the sleeves, her hands were reaching for his belt.

Her eagerness spurred him on. How many nights had he dreamed of this? How many mornings had he awakened remembering her passionate presence in his dreams? But the reality was even more exciting.

They stood facing each other in the soft lamplight, luxuriating in the feeling of discovery and imminent exploration. The light accented Tony's magnificent build and Susan felt her body react to his.

He placed his hands on her waist, then slowly pressed downward until her gown found no more resistance and fell to her feet. Then he slowly leaned down and picked her up in his arms.

"I love you, Susan. But then, you already know that, don't you?"

She nodded, unable to speak. Her heart felt as though it were ready to burst with love for him, but she was unsure how to show it. Suddenly shy, she reached for the sheet when he laid her gently on the bed.

"Are you cold?" he asked, settling down beside her.

"Not really," she murmured.

He leaned up on his elbow and stared down at her. "Are you afraid of me?" he asked, gently pushing a curl behind her ear.

She shook her head. "I'm just not sure what to do. I want to show you my love, but I don't have any experience to fall back on."

He grinned. "That's all right. I'm sure we can find some time to help you gain some experience in this area." His hand slipped down to her breast and lightly stroked it.

She could feel the tension mount in her body. Although her breath seemed to be coming rapidly, her body felt heavy, as though she could hardly move.

He lowered his lips to hers, brushing them in a soft caress, then placed them on her breast. His soft curls brushed against her and she felt a tremor start deep within her, one she couldn't control.

Tony took his time initiating her into the art of making love. He wanted their time together to be perfect for her. He felt her body quicken beneath his loving hands and he patiently guided her into each successive step of intimacy. By the time he moved above her, there was no doubt in either of their minds that she was ready for his possession.

Once again he took his time, adjusting himself to her, kissing her with long, mind-drugging kisses, loving her with every kiss, touch and stroke. He carefully began the rhythmic motions of love. She belonged to him now, and neither of them was likely to forget it after this night.

Susan felt as though she were spiraling ever higher into a black void. She wound her arms tighter around his shoulders and clung, holding him convulsively as a sudden sparkle of showering stars exploded all around her, the brilliant incandescence blinding her to everything but Tony.

He recognized her fulfillment and let go of his fierce control. A final, powerful surge thrust him into the same fiery display of color, and for the first time in months Tony experienced the intense feeling of completion and relaxation that he had willingly given up, hoping to find it only with Susan.

It had been worth the wait.

He rolled to his side, pulling her onto his chest, where she fell into relaxed slumber for the first time in months. With a contented smile Tony joined her. For the first time in years they found peace in each other's arms.

Susan and Tony were at the hospital by six the next morning. They found Hannah asleep in a large chair in the room assigned to Steve, but Steve wasn't there yet.

Hannah woke up at the sound of the door opening and came to her feet, but when she saw who it was she relaxed.

"I thought you were Steve," she explained.

"Have you heard anything?" Susan asked.

"No." She glanced at her watch. "But he should be here within the hour."

"Why don't we go down to the cafeteria and get some breakfast," Tony suggested. "I'll leave word at the nurses' station to call us if they bring him down before we get back."

Neither woman felt like arguing with him and he made sure both of them had full trays before they left the food line.

After her first cup of coffee Hannah studied the couple across the table from her. "Is it my imagination or do you two have some secret sleeping potion? You look much better than I feel this morning."

Tony glanced at Susan and saw a soft flush cover her cheeks. He reached over and took her hand, then smiled at Hannah. "I don't know about Susan, but I'm on top of the world this morning." He squeezed her hand gently. "Susan has agreed to marry me as soon as Steve is well enough to be at the wedding."

"Hallelujah!" Hannah exclaimed. "It's about time somebody woke up around here." Her smile radiated good will. "I couldn't be happier for you both."

"I don't know why I held out for so long," Susan admitted. "Everyone knows Tony's irresistible when he sets his mind on something."

Hannah grinned. "Actually, Steve and I had a bet going that you would be married before Tony left for spring training. I didn't think he'd talk you around quite so soon."

"You mean that's why Steve was so upset when

Tony left? I thought it was because he'd left without telling him good-bye."

"That was part of it, of course. But he'd also made that bet . . . and he lost."

Tony leaned his arms on the table and with amused interest asked, "What was the bet?"

With a great deal of satisfaction Hannah explained, "If he lost the bet, he had to keep his room clean, including vacuuming and scrubbing his bathtub every week without my having to remind him."

Tony and Susan started laughing. "And if he'd won?" Susan finally managed to ask.

Hannah shrugged. "Oh, then I had to make all of his favorite dishes at least once a week. It was a fair bet."

The page interrupted their conversation with "Susan McCormick, please call Extension four two eight."

Susan was out of the chair before the end of the announcement. When she returned to the table, she was smiling. "That was the nurse on Steve's floor. Recovery just called and said they were bringing him down now."

The three of them left the cafeteria and went back upstairs. They were waiting in his room when he was wheeled in.

Even knowing what to expect, the sight of him was still a shock to Susan. There were several tubes running in and out of the covers. And he looked so still. His face was bruised and swollen, and the black stitches stood out in stark relief on his white face.

"Oh, Steve," she whispered. Then she felt Tony's hand take hers and squeeze.

As they transferred Steve to the bed, his eyes fluttered open. "Mom?" His voice sounded sleepy and very weak.

"I'm right here, honey." She stepped over to the bed and picked up his limp hand.

"What happened?"

"What do you remember?"

"I'm not sure. I remember seeing Dr. Masters, and I remember hurting. What did I do?"

"You didn't do anything, darling, except try to get home from school. A car hit you, but you're going to be fine." She fought to keep the tears from filling her eyes.

"I'm very proud of you, Steve," Tony said, walking to the side of the bed by Susan.

Steve's eyes widened in sleepy wonder. "Tony?"

"That's right, son."

"How did you get here so quick?"

Tony's smile was tender. "I'll always be here, whenever you need me."

Steve's eyes drifted closed, then opened once more. He tried to smile, but the effort caused some pain and he gave a soft whimper. "I'm glad." His eyes closed once more.

Tony leaned over and kissed him on his forehead. "So am I, son. So am I."

10

⬦⬦⬦⬦⬦⬦⬦⬦⬦⬦⬦

And here, ladies and gentlemen, to accept the award given by his teammates, coaching staff and the owners of the Atlanta Aces, for sixteen years of outstanding ballplaying, is Tony Antonelli!''

The master of ceremonies led the applause and cheering that reverberated through the huge ball-room of one of Atlanta's most prestigious hotels. Susan had a moment of quiet thankfulness that the traditional head table had been omitted for the evening, so that she didn't feel quite so much on display. She watched Tony thread his way around the large round dinner tables on his way to the podium. He was forced to stop repeatedly as various people patted his back and arms, or grabbed his hands.

Two-year-old Scott stirred in her arms, then relaxed once again. Even if his daddy had caused all the commotion, the day had been too much for him, and he slept peacefully through the excitement. Susan stroked his dark curls away from his forehead with a smile. He looked so much like Tony, but then so did Steve, seated on the other side of four-year-old Tricia. At fifteen, Steve was an exact replica of his father at that age—large and well-built—and already catching the eye of the girls. Only Tricia had taken after her mother. Susan watched as Tricia sat up on her knees so she had a better view of Tony as he stepped up to the podium. Instead of dying down, the noise intensified and he stood there waiting, his famous smile lighting up the room—as well as Susan's heart.

She saw him glance over to their table and wink. Steve made the age-old gesture for "the champ" and they waited for the room to quiet.

Susan felt as though her body were too fragile to contain the burst of love and joy she felt for the man waiting patiently for the noise to subside. Because of his quiet determination and persistence, traits that had helped him forge his way to the top of his field, he had convinced her that they could make their marriage work despite separate careers, almost opposite personalities and circumstances that would have torn most couples apart.

He'd been right.

In the silence of the room Tony began to speak. Steve sat on the edge of his chair, hanging on to every word, his face radiating his pride.

Steve. How blessed they were to have him in good

health. Although his recovery from his accident had been slow, he'd taken his recuperation period very well. Tony helped tremendously with that. She'd never forget the day Tony had had to fly back to Atlanta. He'd stayed for three days, making sure Steve was responding to treatment as expected. The pain had been predictable, but Susan would never forget how helpless she felt just sitting by his side and watching. But Tony seemed to know just what to do, what conversation to make, to keep Steve's mind off his discomfort as much as possible.

"By the way, Steve," Tony mentioned that day in a casual tone, "did your mom tell you she's agreed to marry me?"

"No kidding? Wow, Tony, that's great!" Then he looked over at his mother and frowned. "Why couldn't you've decided before he left, Mom? Then I wouldn't have to be working so hard on my room!"

Susan couldn't help it, she burst out laughing. "Oh, Steve, is that all it means to you?" she finally asked.

He had the grace to blush. "Well, no, not exactly." He looked at Tony very seriously and asked, "When are you going to get married?"

"Well, you've given me some pretty good advice in the past. What do you think?"

"I suppose you wanna marry her right away, huh?"

Tony's eyes danced as he took Susan's hand and laid it against his cheek. "That sounds good to me. I've waited a long time for her, you know."

Steve studied the two of them in silence for a moment. "Yeah, I guess so. You probably want to marry her before you have to leave again, don't you?" His face held no expression, and Susan wasn't sure what that meant. But Tony obviously did.

"Oh, I don't mind waiting until you can be at the ceremony, if that's okay with you."

Steve's eyes lit up and his smile reminded Susan of summer sunshine—bright and sparkling. "Yeah, that'd be super."

"Then you'd better work hard at getting out of here, because I'm going to be counting the days."

Steve tried to straighten up in bed and Susan quickly pulled his pillow into a better position. "You bet, Tony. I can hardly wait. Then you'll be my *real* dad, right?"

Susan's heart lurched into an uncomfortable rhythm and she couldn't say a word.

"That's right, Steve," Tony said softly.

"And then I'll be Steve Antonelli, won't I?" he insisted, and Susan could no long remain silent.

"It doesn't work that way, honey. My name will change, not yours."

"Oh." His crestfallen expression told Susan all she needed to know about Steve's feelings. But he wasn't the only one involved.

Later Tony told her to handle the situation however she felt best, but she understood how painful the reminder was to him. So she had gone to Michael's parents and had a long talk with them. They loved Steve, but they had long since realized his resemblance to Tony. Michael's mother finally made the explanation that summed up how each of them felt.

"Michael loved Steve but he was never a father to him. He was too wrapped up in his music to really notice anyone else. Michael's music was his legacy to the world. But Steve—well, he's a very special legacy, and he belongs to Tony."

So Stephen Spencer McCormick became Stephen Spencer Antonelli as soon after the wedding as adoption papers could be processed.

The wedding. What a riot that had turned out to be! Their marriage took place in July, in the middle of baseball season. They made plans for a small family wedding in Santa Barbara, but it hadn't turned out quite that way.

The manager of Tony's team called Susan and asked them to consider getting married in Atlanta, otherwise his entire team intended to fly out for the wedding, baseball season and scheduled games notwithstanding! None of them intended to miss watching Tony's bachelor downfall.

A quick call to Tony confirmed the manager's concerns—everyone wanted to attend. So Susan spent the last few weeks before their wedding commuting between Atlanta, trying to take care of the arrangements for a large wedding, and Santa Barbara, trying to take care of her law practice. Air travel and the attendant jet-lag became part of her life. But it had been worth it. She'd been surprised to discover she enjoyed all of it—the teasing and confusion, the search for a church and the interviews with the pastor, and the anticipation of becoming, at long last, Mrs. Tony Antonelli.

Her parents flew to Atlanta for the wedding with Hannah and Steve, and Susan gladly yielded the burden of the final preparations to her mother, whose unflappable efficiency quickly dealt with the unexpected last-minute details. Once again, her mother had surprised her, accepting their marriage with quiet dignity.

The Spencers had taken Steve home with them while she and Tony had managed to spend three days completely alone.

As she forced her attention back to the banquet hall, Susan glanced at the sleeping Scott and fidgeting Tricia and ruefully acknowledged that their honeymoon seemed to have been their last time alone.

Tony had been so nervous! The wedding itself had been beautiful, partly because the weather had cooperated and partly because the service had been specially planned by them both. However, Tony had been so pale, Susan was convinced he was coming down with something and had visions of her new husband being fed antibiotics and fever-reducing medication during their entire honeymoon.

Susan had been too busy trying to get her work completed or turned over to other people to have much time to be nervous about the actual ceremony. But poor Tony had been the brunt of innumerable, and mostly unmentionable, practical jokes by his teammates. She wondered later how he had had the nerve to go through with the marriage! She remembered asking him about it when they were finally alone after the ceremony.

"You know I'm too stubborn to give in," he had muttered as he nuzzled her neck.

They were sitting in the living area of their luxurious hotel suite, Susan on Tony's lap on the overlong sofa. She noted that all the while he was making his explanations, his hand was smoothly sliding up and down her leg.

"Are we going to have any dinner?" she asked while he continued to nibble along her neck, his hand now resting on her knee and slowly moving upward.

"Dinner?" he repeated, then raised his head. "You're hungry?" His eyes showed pained disbelief.

In her most pedantic tones Susan explained, "It is very important to the body that it be fueled on a consistent basis. Studies have shown that three meals a day, taken at regular intervals—"

"What a little monster you are!" he exclaimed, grabbing her and sliding down on the sofa beside her. "You can't be hungry after all the food you put away at the reception!"

She feigned surprise. "Oh, I forgot about that. Will my body understand that was supposed to be my dinner?"

Once again his hand crept steadily up her thigh. "I fully intend to educate your body so it understands lots of things."

Her hands slipped through his hair. "I can hardly wait."

Susan was suddenly brought to the present by loud applause. She realized Tony had finished speaking and was returning to sit down beside her once more and she hadn't heard a word he'd said!

"Do you realize you made me lose my train of thought up there?" he whispered as he sat down and the master of ceremonies began speaking again.

"Me?" She looked at him in astonishment.

He grinned. "Who else? I glanced back here and you were staring at me with the most tantalizing smile on your face, the one you get in bed when—"

"Tony!" she gasped, then looked around quickly. Luckily, no one else was close enough to hear him.

"Are you ready to go? There's something about that particular expression on your face that turns my thoughts away from baseball, and everything else. Let's go home!"

As the banquet crowd began to stand and move around, Tony slipped Scott out of her arms, nestling him across his large chest. It was easy to explain that they needed to get home and put the children to bed. Yes, it might have been easier to get a sitter, Tony explained more than once, but he had wanted his entire family with him on the night he officially announced he was retiring from baseball.

It had been his last season and it had been another good one. Once again they'd made it into the World Series, and had won. Once again Tony had won the MVP award. He was proud of his honors, proud of his career, but made it clear to everyone that his family was the culmination of his greatest dreams.

He was waiting in bed for Susan when she walked

out of the bathroom. She'd enjoyed the condominium in Atlanta but knew she wasn't going to miss it once it was sold. The beach house made a very nice full-time residence for them. Her gaze fell on Tony as he lay stretched out on the bed. The covers were already shoved to the bottom and his firmly muscled body lay there, unadorned, in all its glory.

She never grew tired of looking at him—at his wide shoulders and deep chest, his tapered waist and slender hips, his well-developed thighs and hardened calves. But most of all, what really affected her more than anything else was the love shining brightly from his dark eyes.

"Were you waiting for me?" she asked as she slipped off her robe and curled up against him.

"You could say that. I was just thinking about some of the things we used to plan when we were kids."

When they were kids. Steve never grew tired of listening to Tony's anecdotes about how his mother and father met, grew up together, and all the things they did. Even Tricia had a few favorite stories that she liked to hear at bedtime and Tony never seemed to tire of the retelling.

"What plans in particular were you thinking of?" The tip of her tongue teased his earlobe, causing him to shiver slightly.

"Uh, how can I think when you do that?" he muttered, leaning up on his elbow and staring down at her with a mock ferocious expression. She reached up and pulled his head down to hers, kissing him slowly but very thoroughly. When she finally let go of him, she smiled.

"Would you like me to repeat the question?"

"Question?"

"Um-hmm. What plans did we have as kids that you were thinking of?"

"Oh, yes." His mischievous grin made her realize she'd taken the bait—he hadn't forgotten for a moment. "Remember when we were first talking about getting married, and we agreed that someday we would have four children?" All the while he was talking he was slipping the sheer nightgown from Susan, effectively distracting her from the conversation.

"That was a long time ago, Tony."

"I know. You were just a baby then. Now you're a middle-aged matron," he whispered.

"What!" She sat up in bed, incensed.

"What I mean is, I'm sure you feel that three children are more than enough for your nerves, and you're ready to settle down and wait for your grandchildren, right?"

"Tony, for your information, I am only thirty-three years old. That is not middle-aged. That is not time to wait for grandchildren."

"Then what would you say to our having another child in say, oh, nine months or so?"

She leaned back on her pillow, fully aware of his strategy. She assumed a slightly worried frown. "But Tony, let's face it. You've already hit retirement age. Isn't that a little too much to ask of an old man like you?"

The ensuing struggle, amid baritone chuckles and soprano giggles, eventually came to a most satisfying conclusion, disproving all myths about retired baseball players and so-called middle-aged matrons.

If Tony's plans for a larger family didn't work out, it was certainly not from lack of trying and the total cooperation of both parties.

...now read on

Silhouette Special Editions. Longer, more involving stories of real love. And on November the 8th, Silhouette are publishing the Christmas gift pack of four brand new Special Edition romances for just £4.40.

Almost Heaven
CAROLE HALSTON

Remember the Dreams
CHRISTINE FLYNN

Tears in the Rain
PAMELA WALLACE

Water Dancer
JILLIAN BLAKE

Silhouette Desire Romances

TAKE 4
THRILLING SILHOUETTE
DESIRE ROMANCES
ABSOLUTELY FREE

Experience all the excitement, passion and pure joy of love. Discover fascinating stories brought to you by Silhouette's top selling authors. At last an opportunity for you to become a regular reader of Silhouette Desire. You can enjoy 6 superb new titles every month from Silhouette Reader Service, with a whole range of special benefits, a free monthly Newsletter packed with recipes, competitions and exclusive book offers. Plus information on the top Silhouette authors, a monthly guide to the stars and extra bargain offers.

An Introductory FREE GIFT for YOU.
Turn over the page for details.

As a special introduction we will send you FOUR
specially selected Silhouette Desire romances
— yours to keep FREE — when you complete
and return this coupon to us.

At the same time, because we believe that you will be so thrilled
with these novels, we will reserve a subscription to Silhouette
Reader Service for you. Every month you will receive 6 of the very
latest novels by leading romantic fiction authors, delivered direct to
your door.

Postage and packing is always completely
free. There is no obligation or commitment —
you can cancel your subscription at any time.

It's so easy. Send no money now. Simply fill in and post
the coupon today to:-

**SILHOUETTE READER SERVICE, FREEPOST,
P.O. Box 236 Croydon, SURREY CR9 9EL**

Please note: READERS IN SOUTH AFRICA to write to:-
Silhouette, Postbag X3010 Randburg 2125 S. Africa

FREE BOOKS CERTIFICATE

**To: Silhouette Reader Service, FREEPOST, PO Box 236,
Croydon, Surrey CR9 9EL**

Please send me, Free and without obligation, four specially selected Silhouette Desire Romances and reserve a
Reader Service Subscription for me. If I decide to subscribe, I shall, from the beginning of the month following my
free parcel of books, receive six books each month for £5.94, post and packing free. If I decide not to subscribe I
shall write to you within 10 days. The free books are mine to keep in any case. I understand that I may cancel my
subscription at any time simply by writing to you. I am over 18 years of age.
Please write in BLOCK CAPITALS.

Name _____

Address _____

_____

_____ Postcode _____

SEND NO MONEY — TAKE NO RISKS
Remember postcodes speed delivery. Offer applies in U.K. only
and is not valid to present subscribers. Silhouette reserve the right
to exercise discretion in granting membership. If price changes
are necessary you will be notified.
Offer limited to one per household. Offer expires April 30th, 1986.

EP18SD